"You're all heart,"

Liz said as she reached for a diaper. "It's made of stone, but you're all heart."

"How would you know what my heart's made of?" Griff demanded.

She deposited the wet diaper into the blue pail and glanced over her shoulder. "Well, for one thing, you didn't kiss me before. You wanted to, though."

If ever a woman deserved the label Impossible, it was her. "I also wanted to strangle you a minute ago, but I didn't do that, either."

"Murder's against the law," she told him as she expertly tucked and secured the new diaper onto the baby's bottom. "Kissing isn't."

"Maybe it's against mine."

"Laws are made to protect people."

"Exactly."

She turned, a challenge in her eyes. "Are you afraid of me?"

He should have just ignored her, should have just taken his niece and driven away. Instead, he met her challenge head-on.

Dear Reader:

Happy July! It's a month for warm summer evenings, barbecues and—of course—the Fourth of July. It's a time of enjoyment and family gatherings. It's a time for romance!

The fireworks are sparkling this month at Silhouette Romance. Our DIAMOND JUBILEE title is *Borrowed Baby* by Marie Ferrarella, a heartwarming story about a brooding loner who suddenly becomes a father when his sister leaves him with a little bundle of joy! Then, next month, don't miss *Virgin Territory* by Suzanne Carey. Dedicated bachelor Phil Catterini is determined to protect the virtue of Crista O'Malley—and she's just as determined to change her status as "the last virgin in Chicago." Looks like his bachelorhood will need the protection instead as these two lovers go hand in hand into virgin territory.

The DIAMOND JUBILEE—Silhouette Romance's tenth anniversary celebration—is our way of saying thanks to you, our readers. To symbolize the timelessness of love, as well as the modern gift of the tenth anniversary, we're presenting readers with a DIAMOND JUBILEE Silhouette Romance title each month, penned by one of your favorite Silhouette Romance authors. In the coming months, writers such as Annette Broadrick, Lucy Gordon, Dixie Browning and Phyllis Halldorson are writing DIAMOND JUBILEE titles especially for you.

And that's not all! There are six books a month from Silhouette Romance—stories by wonderful authors who time and time again bring home the magic of love. During our anniversary year, each book is special and written with romance in mind. July brings you *Venus de Molly* by Peggy Webb—a sequel to her heartwarming *Harvey's Missing*. The second book in Laurie Paige's poignant duo, *Homeward Bound*, is coming your way in July. Don't miss *Home Fires Burning Bright*—Carson and Tess's story. And much-loved Diana Palmer has some special treats in store in the month ahead. Don't miss Diana's fortieth Silhouette—*Connal*. He's a LONG, TALL TEXAN out to lasso your heart, and he'll be available in August....

I hope you'll enjoy this book and all of the stories to come. Come home to romance—Silhouette Romance—for always!

Sincerely,

Tara Hughes Gavin
Senior Editor

MARIE FERRARELLA

Borrowed Baby

Silhouette Romance

Published by Silhouette Books New York

America's Publisher of Contemporary Romance

This book is dedicated
to the memory of Jack Teal,
a very fine gentleman,
and to
Liz Lax and her Casie
for inspiring it all.

SILHOUETTE BOOKS
300 E. 42nd St., New York, N.Y. 10017

ISBN: 0-373-08730-6

First Silhouette Books printing July 1990

Printed in the U.S.A.

MARIE FERRARELLA

was born in Europe, raised in New York City and now lives in Southern California. The tired mother of two overenergetic children and contented wife of one wonderful man is thrilled to be following her dream of writing full-time.

A Note From The Author:

Dear Reader,

They used to say that love makes the world go around, and I for one truly believe that. Silhouette Romances are about love and about people. Silhouette Romances have been a part of our lives now for ten years. Imagine, ten years. There's something so solid about such a round number. I have a fondness for round numbers. This is my twentieth novel for Silhouette Books. That's something that makes me want to celebrate, too.

Writing for Silhouette Books is special to me. What I love best about writing Silhouette Romances is that they allow me to recapture the thrill of my own romance— those precious early days when significant glances were exciting and rooms melted away at the hint of a kiss and there was no laundry to do. I love writing about that. I love reliving that. I hope you feel that way about reading my novels.

Sincerely,

Marie Ferrarella

Chapter One

The last thing in the world that Elizabeth Ann MacDougall had on her mind that fateful brisk Thursday afternoon was a stop sign. It wasn't part of her hastily conceived plan.

She had just picked up Alec from his first-grade class. Alec's teacher, Ms. Giles, was not one of those educators who immediately threw open the doors at the sound of the dismissal bell. She was dedicated. There were, it seemed, always last-minute instructions to be heaped upon their six-year-old, incredibly short attention spans.

Today, it appeared, Ms. Giles was outdoing herself. Liz, whose life was usually planned down to the second, had not allotted herself time for the extra few minutes that it took Alec to finally emerge from the classroom, wet watercolor clutched in his hand.

"Look, Whiz. Alec," Winston pointed out eagerly.

"Yes," Liz assured the three-year-old as she forged forward. "I recognize him."

Grabbing Alec and herding Bruce and Nathan before her while she held on to Winston, she piled the boys into her dusty yellow Honda. Peter, the baby, chose that moment to wake up and howl his displeasure at being left confined in his car seat, never mind that he had slept through the whole ordeal of waiting for the boys to appear.

A shortcut home was her only way out. She turned the car around.

Liz snaked her way past the countless cars and vans that made precarious pit stops before the sprawling, one-story suburban school and took the back road out. She barely missed having a blue VW bus become intimately involved with her rear bumper.

"Made it," she breathed, and clenched her teeth. From here on in, it should be smooth sailing.

Her words were drowned out by the fight that suddenly flared up in the back seat over who had scored the most points in yesterday's GI Joe battle.

"Boys, it doesn't matter who scored the most points, remember?"

They obviously didn't, because the argument, complete with new, imaginative titles for each of the participants, continued. These were soon followed by screams. By now, she was becoming pretty astute at discerning which scream was serious and which was just for effect. Still, the noise was disconcerting while she was trying to concentrate on the road. That, plus

the fact that there remained only six crucial minutes
before the timer in her kitchen went off, did not ren-
der Liz in the most lucid frame of mind. She wasn't
quite as alert as she should have been. Oh, she could
have averted a collision with an oncoming truck. But
the stop sign was a lot smaller. Also sneakier.

It just seemed to pop out of nowhere as she pulled
out of the school road and onto the main thoroughfare. She caught sight of it out of the corner of her eye
just as she eased the car onto the semiempty road.

Jamming her foot down on the brake, she stopped,
then went on, both satisfied and relieved that there was
nothing around that could hit her or impede her
progress back to her house.

A bloodcurdling scream rose from the back seat. Liz
tightened her hands on the wheel. "Alec, you know
Bruce bites when you provoke him." She didn't have
to turn around to know what was happening. She just
knew. "You shouldn't have put your hand in front of
his face like that."

The indignant grunt told her that Alec was retaliat-
ing. Some days, Liz thought with an inward sigh, were
worse than others. This was definitely going down as
a "worse."

The only silent one in the car was Peter. She glanced
in his direction and saw that he was continuing to
drool onto her upholstery as he shoved his fist into his
mouth.

Liz blew her blond bangs up from her eyes and
made a turn into her development, grateful that it was
right down the road from the school. Just as she made
the turn, she realized that one of the children was

trying to get her attention. It was Winston. He probably wanted to know what there was to eat once they
got home. Winston *always* wanted to know what there
was to eat.

"What is it, Winston?" She tried to sound patient.

But this time, the boy's question had nothing to do
with food, only colors. "What do whirling red and
blue lights mean?"

With a sinking feeling quickly spreading in the pit
of her stomach, Liz looked up into the rearview mirror. Sure enough, the lights were there, swirling and
dancing. They were attached to an ominous police car.

Liz's shoulders sagged beneath her denim jacket.
"About fifty-five dollars," she answered with a sigh.
"All this and heaven too." There was nothing left to
do but pull over to the side and wait.

The argument in the back seat evaporated as the
boys craned their necks to be the first to see what was
going to happen next.

"Wow, a police car." Bruce clambered to his knees
on top of Alec's hand. "Are we going to jail?" The
possibility clearly thrilled him.

Alec shoved him off. "I told you not to bite me,"
the older boy taunted. "Now you'll get it."

No, Liz thought in despair, only me.

It seemed to Liz that the policeman was taking forever to reach her car. Probably part of their training
to unnerve their victims. In her mind's eye, she saw her
cake going from golden brown to charcoal. Served her
right for trying to juggle too many things at once.
Someday, she was going to learn to take things slowly

and do them one at a time. Of course, that didn't help
the situation right now, but it was food for thought.

Officer Griffin Foster was not in the best of moods.
His disposition could more aptly be described as akin
to that of a wounded bear. It was an hour before his
tour of duty would be over and he was more than
ready to go home. He had been traveling down Jef-
frey Road trying to understand how a single nine-inch
taco, consumed in a rush three hours ago, could be
making every inch of his six-foot-three frame suffer
this way. His was not a stomach that could tolerate
Mexican food that came from a place that promised
"meals in a minute," he thought with resignation.

He was just becoming acquainted with the true
meaning of the word *heartburn* when he had spotted
the yellow Honda sliding past the stop sign and out
onto the street.

Another California stop. Another housewife rushing off somewhere without regard to the proper rules
of the road. Didn't they ever stop to think what one
misstep could cost them?

Griff had shaken his head as he'd followed the car,
throwing the switch that brought the lights on the roof
of his squad car to life. The errant driver had kept
going. Obviously the woman hadn't bothered to look
into her rearview mirror, either. He had been about to
engage the siren when the driver had finally slowed
down and pulled over at the entrance to the development. He'd thought it rather a dark twist of fate that
it should be his development. So near and yet so far.
He thought longingly of the antacid tablets in his
medicine cabinet.

Duty first. Griff got out of the car and slowly walked over to the yellow Honda, bracing himself for the onslaught of breathless, imaginative excuses that usually met him when he pulled over a careless driver.

Liz watched the tall policeman in the navy blue uniform approach in her side mirror. His uniform looked as if it were molded to his body. How did these men even breathe? she wondered. He was the picture of a solemn, unsmiling giant. Even his mustache looked as if it were frowning. Probably because he couldn't get in enough air.

There was no talking her way out of this one, she thought in resignation.

"May I see your license?"

His voice matched the rest of him, Liz thought. Deep, forbidding. As she pulled her wallet from her purse she wondered if he knew how to smile. Liz flipped to her license and offered it up to him.

He made no move to take it. "Take it out of the wallet, please."

That struck her as odd. "Aren't you allowed to handle wallets?" she asked.

He wondered if he had a wise guy on his hands. "Just take it out, please," he repeated.

Liz forced a smile to her lips. The man probably has a heart of stone, she thought. She passed the license to him and waited for the inevitable ticket.

Griff looked down at the license and absently noted that she lived on Chambers Street. Six blocks away from his house. He looked back at her face. She looked unfamiliar, but that wasn't all that unusual. For the most part, although he had lived in the development for almost four years, he kept to himself. He wasn't into socializing.

Liz wondered why he was studying her so intently. Was he trying to decide just how much trouble she was in? How much trouble *was* she in? She almost asked, but then the boys took over.

"Are you going to take us to jail, Mr. Policeman?" Bruce asked eagerly.

Griff looked into the back seat and saw that it was filled to overflowing with children. He looked at Liz in mild surprise. She looked awfully young to have so many.

"No," he answered, his tone expressionless. He turned his attention back to Liz. "Did you see that stop sign back there?"

He'd make a wonderful interrogator, she thought. Probably had ancestors that went back to the Spanish Inquisition. Where was he when Alec's bicycle had been stolen from in front of her very door? She decided that it was prudent not to bring the matter up.

"Yes, I did," she answered brightly. She gave him her most confident look. "I stopped." It never hurt to try.

Griff's brows drew together as another surge of heartburn attacked him. "You slid," he corrected.

God, he looked angry. Heart of stone, just as she predicted. "I slid," she admitted. She reached toward the glove compartment. "Do you want to see my registration?" That was usually step two before the dreaded ticket materialized, or so she had heard. This was to be her very first ticket and she was more than a little distressed about it.

Griff glanced again into the back seat. She must really have her hands full all day long, he thought. He saw her hesitate as she reached for the glove compartment. "Why?" he asked. "Did you steal the car?"

She looked down at Peter's drool marks on the upholstery. "If I was going to steal a car, it wouldn't be a compact." She saw him raise his eyebrow questioningly. Terrific, now he thinks you're contemplating stealing cars. "No, I didn't," she said quietly.

She looked honest enough, just slightly harried. "Then I don't need to see your registration."

He didn't normally make exceptions. That wasn't his style. But every once in a while, it didn't hurt to look the other way. And if there was ever a woman who needed a little leeway, it was this blue-eyed, honey blonde. She made him think of the woman in the shoe, except that she was a lot younger and prettier than anything he'd picture in a nursery rhyme book.

"Here."

Liz stared at his hand as he offered her back her license. After a beat, she took it from him. This didn't make any sense. "Aren't you going to give me a ticket?"

"Do you want one?"

"No, of course not, but..." Her voice trailed off as she looked up at him, confused.

Griff allowed a small smile to appear beneath the trim, dark brown mustache. "Lady, you look like you've already got enough trouble, what with four kids—"

"Four?" Her brows jumped together as her head swung around, the freshly made ponytail slicing the air as she turned. "I had five when I started out."

"Get off me, Nathan!" a muffled voice cried. Winston.

She turned back around. "Five," she asserted, relieved.

"Five," Griff echoed dubiously and shook his head. He had thought the day of the large family had gone. After seeing this family in action, he could well understand why that particular setup was becoming extinct.

He tipped his hat and took a step back from her car. "Drive carefully."

She grinned at him. The man had a heart after all. You learn something everyday. "Definitely," she promised with a wink.

That wink was most likely what had gotten her pregnant in the first place, he thought. It had "sexy" written all over it. Her husband probably couldn't keep his hands off her. Not that he blamed him. Looking somewhat apprehensive and harried, there was still something captivatingly attractive about the woman.

Griff turned and walked back to his car. Seating himself behind the steering wheel, he watched and waited for her to pull away.

Liz waved at him, feeling almost giddy at the reprieve. Then, turning on her ignition again, she was on her way, ready to rescue her about-to-be-burnt cake. The argument in the back seat had resumed, but she barely paid any attention.

Griff shook his head. He must be getting soft in his old age. Either that or the taco had gone to his brain and done serious damage. Muttering a disparaging comment, Griff turned his patrol car toward the station off Jamboree. He rubbed his stomach, making small, concentric circles with his large hand. It didn't help.

Under normal circumstances, he would have given the woman a ticket even if she had so many children that she had to strap them to the roof of her car. Maybe he was just having an off day. Or maybe it was the fact that her eyes reminded him of Sally. Not the shade so much as the wide-eyed innocence. Of course, a woman with five children could hardly be called innocent by any stretch of the imagination.

What the hell, one ticket wouldn't make or break the department and it wasn't as if she had flagrantly disregarded the stop sign. Rolling stops were just possibly the main source of revenue in Bedford. Overlooking one was no big deal.

Still, he was surprised at himself. He had never looked the other way before. He believed in rules and regulations. That was why he had become a policeman in the first place. Without structure, without order, there was nothing, he reminded himself as he pulled up in front of the precinct. Everyone needed structure in their lives, even if they had nothing else.

Nodding at several officers on their way out, Griff walked into the newly constructed building adjacent to the new city hall. The city had only been incorporated for eighteen years. Everything was new in Bedford. Only he felt old. An odd way to be at twenty-seven, he thought darkly as fragments from his past came and went through his mind.

"Hey, Griff, why so glum? Couldn't find anyone speeding today?" C. W. Linquist called out as Griff walked by him on the way to the locker room.

"Nope, just another peaceful day in paradise," Griff quipped.

C.W. followed him into the locker room. The sound of running water was heard from the shower area as officers coming off duty prepared to meet more pleasurable challenges that evening.

C.W. nodded toward the showers. "Hey, how about joining Ernie and me tonight? Ernie found a great singles' club. We're trying it on for size right after we grab a bite to eat. Might find something there to take the starch out of your mustache." C.W. nudged him. Five years older and a full six inches shorter, C.W.'s elbow dug into Griff's waist.

Griff opened his locker and took out the shirt he had left hanging there. "I like my mustache starched, C.W. Thanks just the same."

He stripped off his uniform shirt and tossed it into his duffel bag. Griff saw C.W. looking at the taut, muscular torso with unabashed envy. While the rest of them indulged in pizza, Griff spent his time in the gym.

C.W. straddled the bench as he pulled off his shoes and dropped them into his locker with a thud. "C'mon, Griff. I never see you go out with the ladies. Don't you ever like to cut loose?"

Griff tucked his fresh shirt into the waistband of his jeans. "No, it takes the edge off."

"Someday, fella," C.w. predicted, "that edge is going to slice you in half."

Griff didn't care to be analyzed, especially not when he was suffering with hearburn. "Well, then that'll be my concern, won't it?" He picked up his bag and headed toward the door.

"You know your problem?" C.W. called after him. "You think life's too serious."

Griff stopped at the double doors and turned to look over his shoulder at the slightly overweight, red-headed policeman. "Well, isn't it?"

C.W. shook his head. "No, it's what you make it, Griff."

"Yes," Griff agreed, leaving. "It is."

He supposed that he could have gone along with C.W. and Ernie, Griff thought as he drove home. After all, the man didn't mean any harm. He was just trying to be friendly. But being friendly didn't really have a place in Griff's life. He wasn't certain that he even knew *how* to be friendly anymore. Polite, yes. Civil, definitely, but friendly? Spending an evening exchanging small talk about trivialities that neither person really cared about? That was just a waste of his time, a waste of effort. And he had wasted far too much effort trying to make contact in his lifetime, had tried too hard and wouldn't think about trying again.

He learned his lessons well.

It was growing dark earlier and earlier now that Christmas was drawing near. Hardly four o'clock and dusk was quickly approaching. He thought again of the woman he had failed to ticket today. C.W. would probably have tried to make a little time with her, undoubtedly flirting outrageously. C.W. wouldn't be hampered by the fact that the woman was obviously married and the mother of four, no *five*, Griff corrected himself, remembering the muffled voice that called out from beneath one of the other boys.

Why would someone so young want to tie herself down with so many kids? he wondered.

Love, a small voice within him seemed to whisper.

Griff's thoughts came to an abrupt halt. Where had that come from? He would have thought that he'd grown sufficiently past notions like that. Besides, that many kids didn't mean love—it meant pandemonium.

He drove into his development and found himself taking the long road toward his block. Curiosity prompted him to drive down Chambers Street. He saw the dusty yellow Honda parked in the driveway. He slowed down then drove on. There was no reason to hurry. There was nothing waiting for him at home. Nothing and no one. No attachments. And that was just the way he wanted it.

His life was exactly the way he wanted it. He was aware that he stated the fact to himself a bit too emphatically, but dismissed it.

When he turned onto his block and neared his tidy, three-bedroom house, he was surprised to see that there was someone standing on his front steps, waiting. At first glance, he thought it might be the woman he had stopped, but he rejected the idea as being absurd. She had no way of knowing where he lived. Besides, there was no reason for her to seek him out. He hadn't given her a ticket.

He squinted slightly. The fading light made it difficult to distinguish the figure at first. And then...

The last fifteen feet to his driveway unfolded in slow motion as he suddenly recognized the person standing before his house.

Sally.

After all this time. Sally.

For a moment, he was transported back in time. Once again, it was just Sally and Griff, Griff and Sally. Two against the world. Tough odds, but he had beaten them. He had managed to keep them together, from foster home to foster home.

As far back as he could remember, he was all that Sally had had. And she was all he had.

Vaguely, he remembered a limp-looking woman with tired eyes watching as a man beat him. He remembered biting his lip not to cry, not to cry so that Sally wouldn't be afraid. And then a tall, pretty lady who smiled and smelled of soap had come and taken him and Sally away, down a long, dim corridor. The beatings stopped after that. So did the rage and the hurt. And all the feelings. All but one. Protectiveness. He always felt that he had to protect Sally. She was so little. And she cried so easily. But she stopped crying when he sang to her. And she believed him when he said that things would get better. No matter what, Sally always believed.

Only he didn't.

Griff pulled up short and was out of the car, walking like a man in a daze. "Sally?"

The petite brunette nodded, flashing a brave smile. "Surprise." The small mouth trembled and the smile dissolved as tears suddenly formed. "Oh, Griff, I don't have anywhere to go!"

Griff put his arms around the sobbing girl he hadn't seen in two years and held his sister close. "Yes, you do. You're home."

But as he held her, he became aware that there was something between them, something Sally was holding. It squealed. Griff moved back abruptly as if he had been burned.

Sally was holding a baby.

Griff stared down at the bundle, dumbfounded. "Um, when did—?"

Sally pulled back the blanket from the child's face. "Six months ago. Griff," she said, her hopeful eyes on his face, "this is your niece, Cassandra."

It took Griff a full minute before the shock had passed and he could speak again. "Sally, we've got a lot of talking to do."

Chapter Two

Griff unlocked the front door feeling both sad and apprehensive. And angry. A baby. How could she have gotten herself into this much trouble? Glancing over his shoulder, he noticed that Sally stood in the open doorway, looking a little uncertain. The anger softened. "Nothing's changed since you left," he assured her.

He set down Sally's single suitcase and the infant seat next to the living-room sofa they had picked out together. "Traveling light, aren't you?"

Sally took a deep breath and appeared to slowly absorb the surroundings. Her face seemed to relax a little as she smiled sadly. "I haven't acquired too much since I last saw you."

Griff looked dubiously at the baby she cradled against her hip. "Oh, I wouldn't say that." He watched Sally move around the room, touching, absorbing, obviously remembering. She looked a lot thinner. The baby gurgled. Griff's thoughts returned to the infant. "Was it the guitar player?"

His sister swung around. Her arm tightened around her daughter. "His name is Buddy." Sally raised her small chin defensively.

"His name is mud from where I stand." He saw the tension return to her face and reach her shoulders. They weren't going to get anywhere arguing, he told himself. It was enough that she was back. Griff raised his hands to call a truce. "Okay, we'll drop it for now. Hungry?"

Sally looked relieved that he had changed the subject. She nodded her head.

Griff grinned. "I can still boil a mean frozen dinner pouch."

Sally laughed, obviously remembering that it was practically the only kind of meal they had ever had. "Anything," she said.

Griff looked down at the baby. He still couldn't bring himself to accept that it was hers. Part of him, he knew, still thought of Sally as a baby. "How about, um—?" He nodded toward the infant.

"Casie," Sally supplied quickly. "Cassandra's kind of a big name for her," she admitted, "but she'll grow into it. Buddy picked it out."

"It figures," Griff muttered.

Sally acted as if she hadn't heard. "I have everything she needs right here." Sally patted the oversize weather-beaten tan purse that hung from her shoulder. "Don't worry, she'll let us know when she's hungry."

"Swell. C'mon." He led the way into the kitchen. Shifting Casie higher on her hip, Sally picked up the infant seat and followed him.

"You really haven't changed anything." Sally looked around the small kitchen with its light blue wallpaper. Tiny flowers networking their way up the walls gave the kitchen a warm feeling. She and Griff had spent a lot of time in this room, talking. Sally set the infant seat down on the table and strapped Casie into it.

"I didn't have to. I liked everything the way it was." He opened the freezer and took out a Chinese entrée that promised heaven in a transparent pouch. Griff pulled out a pot from the cupboard and filled it with water. He kept his silence long enough to place the pot on a front burner and turn up the heat beneath it. Then he turned and looked at his sister.

"So what happened?"

Sally didn't meet his gaze right away. Instead, she nervously played with the ruffle on Casie's dress. "You mean lately, or in the past two years?"

Griff crossed his arms before his chest and leaned back against the sink. "Any way you want to tell it."

She shrugged, and he thought that she looked more like a baby than her daughter did, if that were possible. She looked so young, so lost. She was only twenty-one. Old enough, obviously, to have a child, and yet not nearly old enough for this kind of responsibility. She was as young as he was old.

"It started out pretty terrific," she said, her voice small.

"But—?"

Sally shot Griff a defiant look. "I know what you're thinking, but Buddy loves me."

Griff looked pointedly at Casie. "Obviously."

"Don't get sarcastic, Griff," Sally pleaded.

He realized that she needed him to understand. Just as he always had. Griff struggled to keep his temper and the explosive words that formed in his mind from falling off the tip of his tongue. "I wasn't being sarcastic, I was contemplating justifiable homicide."

Sally looked away. "Buddy's just having trouble coping with all this. The baby, me, his career not going anywhere."

"Good excuses." Griff's voice was cold, as was the fury he felt against his sister's lover. "And so he walked out on you."

"Kinda."

He straightened and crossed over to her until he was directly behind her chair. "What's that supposed to mean?" For a moment, his hand hovered over her head, wanting to stroke it, wanting to make everything all right. But he let his hand drop. He couldn't afford to let his emotions cloud his judgment. That was a luxury that belonged to other people, not to him.

"It means I'm not sure."

"He left his clothes?"

"No."

"His guitar?"

"Look—" Sally's voice rose "—will you stop being a cop?"

"I thought I was being your big brother."

"Sorry." She looked down at the hands on her lap. She was clasping and unclasping them, as if trying to grab hold of something to make her strong. "You're right, I'm wrong."

Griff turned back to the stove. The water was boiling madly, spilling over the top of the pot and creating billows of steam as it contacted the red-hot burner. He turned down the heat and reached for tongs to fish out the pouch of food. He forced himself to smile. "Well, at least you've learned a little good sense since you've been gone. I accept your apology. Let's start over."

Cutting open the bag, he poured out the contents on a plate. Steam rose and left an airy trail as he brought the plate over to her.

Sally bit her lower lip. "I wasn't sure if I'd still find you here."

Griff placed a fork in front of her and then straddled the chair next to her. "Where would I go? This is our home, remember?"

"It's your home."

"No, it's *ours*," he emphasized, a touch of annoyance in his voice. "I bought it for us. So that we could be like normal people. Remember? Those were your words." He pointed to her plate. "Now eat before your dinner gets cold."

Sally laughed. "You sound like a mother hen." Her expression softened. She reached across the table and placed her hand over his, her fingers curving. "Griff?"

"Yeah?"

"I love you."

He became aware of his heartburn again. It suddenly seemed to have returned with a vengeance. He stood up. "I'll get your room ready."

"Sentiment still embarrass you?"

"Just eat before you waste away." He left the room.

The insistent whimpering grew louder until it finally penetrated Griff's consciousness and forced him to open his eyes. He rolled over in bed and looked bleary-eyed at the glowing red numbers on the digital clock that sat on the nightstand. It took him over a minute to focus in. Four o'clock.

What *was* that sound?

And then it came back to him. Sally. The baby. That was it. The baby was crying.

He sighed and sank back on his pillow. She'd take care of whatever it was that was ailing the kid.

The crying persisted.

How could something so small make so much noise? Maybe there was something wrong. He threw off the covers with a resigned sigh. Once he was awake, there was no going back to sleep. He might as well see if Sally needed help. As he rose, he automatically tugged up the cutoff shorts he always wore to bed, even on the coldest nights. Somehow, pajamas were too restricting to him. The only restrictions he accepted were ones he made for himself.

Groggily he rubbed the sleep from his eyes and shuffled down the hall to the room that had once been his sister's. When she left, he had kept it just the way it was. This house had been Griff's one last stab at normalcy. He had bought it with hopes of giving Sally a real home and, at the same time, giving himself one as well. He had intended on going on with his work on the force, and she was going to graduate from high school and attend college. She was going to become someone, and they were going to beat the odds against them.

The American dream, he thought cynically.

That had been the plan. But plans, he had learned time and again, often found a way to go awry. He should have seen it coming. He was enough of a realist to have been alert to the dangers of dreaming. Sally had fallen in love with a would-be rock star and suddenly he and Sally couldn't carry on a conversation anymore without shouting. The arguments had grown more and more heated the more he tried to show her the error of her ways.

The last time he had seen her, two years ago, she had been on the back of her boyfriend's motorcycle, heading off for parts unknown.

Well, all that was behind them now. Maybe he could somehow make up for lost time. He knocked on her door. "Sally, is everything all right?"

No answer met his question, except for the baby's wail. Inexplicable fear rose up to his throat, where it was wont to lodge when he couldn't put a name on things. "Sally, are you all right?"

Still nothing.

He tried the doorknob and discovered that the door was unlocked. He pushed it open. The room was illuminated by the lamp that stood next to her bed. Sally's bed hadn't been slept in. On top of the covers lay the baby in her infant seat, thrashing about, her arms waving to and fro. Next to her was a note.

He didn't want to think about it.

"Sally?" he called out again, hoping that this wasn't what it looked like.

Casie stopped crying for a moment and seemed to be listening to the sound of his voice.

Griff rushed into the room. The bathroom door was open but the room was empty. She was gone. Why?

He sank down on the bed. The infant seat tipped in his direction. Mechanically, he stopped it without looking at Casie. He picked up the note. It took him a few minutes before he could get himself to read the words.

Dear Griff,
Please try to understand. I have to sort things out for myself. I realized last night that I can't let you do it for me. And I can't do it with Casie. It wouldn't be fair to her. Please take care of her for me, she deserves better than me. So do you.
Love,
Sally

"Damn!"

He crumpled the note and threw it on the floor.

All through her childhood and adolescence, Sally had left messes for him to straighten out.

"This is a little more serious than an unmade bed, Sally," he called out in frustration, addressing the emptiness. "Just what in hell am I supposed to do with her?"

Casie gave a little cry. Griff sighed and stared down at the baby in bewilderment. "What am I supposed to do with you?" Casie's lower lip trembled, but the crying stopped. She seemed intrigued with the sound of his voice. "Take you in the squad car and have you ride shotgun?" Casie answered him in strange noises. Griff threw up his hands. "Great, just great. Not fair to Casie. How fair is it to leave her with me?" he complained angrily. "I don't know the first thing about babies."

Casie laughed, her eyes bright and fixed on Griff. For a second, he almost felt as if she understood. "It's not going to work, kid. I haven't got the faintest idea what to do with you."

What *was* he going to do?

He thought of calling in sick, but they were in the middle of a flu epidemic and already operating at only three-fourths capacity. Besides, taking the day off wouldn't solve anything. This wiggling inconvenience in a pink dress would still be here tomorrow.

There was no one he could turn to. His sphere of acquaintances contained only bachelors. There was no kindly captain's wife to take his niece to, no friendly neighborhood mother to offer her services.

Unless...

He thought of the woman with the carload of children he had stopped yesterday. Didn't she live close by? Maybe she could be prevailed upon to help. He knew he was grasping at straws, but he was three steps past worried, on his way to desperate. What was her address? He wished he had given her a ticket, then at least he'd have her address in his book.

It took him several minutes to remember. When he did, the feeling of triumph quickly dissipated as he realized that he was going to have to ask a stranger for help. But there was no other way.

He made up his mind just as Casie began to whimper again. "Okay, kid, I think I might have found someone to take care of you, at least for today. Maybe I can find your mother by tonight."

Holding the infant seat in place to keep it from tipping again, he rose and began to leave. He turned, noting that Casie's wide blue eyes followed him. As the distance between them grew, so did her whimpers, until a wail burst forth. Griff crossed back to her. The whimpering subsided. "Look, I'm just going to get dressed, okay?"

But as he began to move away, Casie started to cry again.

He sighed in exasperation as he ran his hand through his hair. "Not okay."

He hesitated for a moment, then shrugged, defeated. He scooped Casie up, infant seat and all. "Okay, but keep your eyes shut, you hear? Otherwise, you're going to wind up getting an education and seeing things that you've got no business seeing for at least another twenty years." He looked down at the wide, innocent blue eyes. She seemed to be listening to every word he said, even though he knew that was preposterous. "Maybe longer."

With a sigh, he lugged the infant seat and Casie back to his bedroom.

* * *

Liz had just bounced out of bed and had poured her
first cup of life-giving coffee from the preset coffee
machine when she heard the doorbell ring. She
glanced at the kitchen clock on the wall behind her.
No, she wasn't behind schedule. Someone was early.
But who could be calling at six-thirty in the morning?

Hurrying over to the front door, she looked through
the peephole and saw a policeman standing on her
front step. *The* policeman. What was he doing here at
this hour? And how on earth did he know where she
lived? He must have remembered her address from
checking over her license. Had he changed his mind
about giving her a ticket? Could he do that?

Liz quickly undid the lock, her curiosity consum-
ing her. It intensified when she saw the baby he was
holding.

He wasn't prepared to see her like this. Griff forgot
what he was going to say. When she opened the door,
Griff's eyes involuntarily slid over Liz's slender body.
She was wearing a football jersey that obviously
hadn't once belonged to the biggest man on the team.
More than likely, it had belonged to the smallest. The
navy blue jersey barely skimmed the tops of her
thighs. Firm thighs from what he could see. Probably
kept in shape dashing after that gang of boys of hers.

She was a lot taller than he expected her to be, but
then, he had only seen her sitting down. Her honey-
blond hair was loose, framing her diamond-shaped
face. She looked like the cheerleader type. Not just any
cheerleader. Head cheerleader. It wasn't that she
looked empty-headed or vain, just perky, incredibly

perky, considering the hour. If he hadn't known better, he'd have thought that she was lifted directly from a soft drink commercial and deposited in front of him.

He found himself uncomfortable around her and wasn't certain if it was because he had to ask a favor of a stranger or because she was decidedly underdressed for the occasion and he was having a very basic, very male reaction to her.

Startled though she was to see him, Liz was aware that the policeman was giving her the once-over. She wondered if she passed. She couldn't tell. He had a wide, rugged face that gave absolutely no clues as to what was going on behind those large brown eyes.

What on earth was he doing here?

Casie yelped as Griff shifted her seat.

"Arresting them a little young, aren't you?"

Griff cleared his throat. Though he tried to hide it, his discomfort was evident. He raised the infant seat and infant slightly in the air. "This is my niece."

Liz inclined her head. That still didn't explain what he was doing here. He certainly hadn't brought the child over for show-and-tell. If she was any judge, he looked as if he didn't even like holding the little girl.

"Hello, Niece." Liz assessed the awkward way he was holding the baby, almost at arm's length—and he had long arms. "You're holding her as if you expect her to explode at any second."

He didn't think he liked her attitude. "Do you always answer the door at six-thirty half naked?"

Maybe he came here to pick a fight. "I don't usually answer the door at six-thirty at all." A breeze threatened to separate her from all attempts at mod-

esty. Her hand darted down to the hem of the jersey.
"Get in here. It's downright chilly outside."

She took hold of his arm, intending to draw him in.
It was a purely reflexive move. He didn't budge. His
arm felt hard, unyielding beneath her hand. Liz
looked at him curiously, mild amusement highlight-
ing the corners of her mouth. "Does this come under
the heading of assaulting an officer?"

Only then did he take a step inside her house. "I,
um, have a problem."

"Yes," she agreed, closing the door, "you definitely do." Taking pity on him, Liz took the disgruntled baby out of his hands. She could feel the
dampness even with the baby strapped into the seat.
"She's wet," Liz accused.

Griff nodded. "That's part of the problem."

"Why didn't you change her?"

"I, um—" In response, he held out the purse Sally
had left behind. "I think there are things you need in
here."

"Another man afraid of diapers. C'mon, follow
me." She led him to the family room.

They stepped across a maze comprised of toys and
games. She set Casie down on the sofa and un-
strapped her. Pushing the baby seat aside, she reached
her hand up toward Griff without looking. "Diaper,
please."

Griff felt as if he were involved in some kind of rit-
ualistic surgery. "Here." He gave her what he assumed was a diaper. It was square and covered in
white plastic and didn't look a thing like cloth.

Deftly, Liz began to change the baby. She noticed with amusement that the policeman averted his eyes as she did so. The man was definitely one for the books.

"There, nice and dry. At least for the moment." She sat the infant up and smoothed down the frilly pink dress. "She certainly is a cutie. Does she have a name?"

"Who?"

Liz looked over her shoulder at the policeman. She was five foot seven and she still felt dwarfed by him. Liz rose to her feet, taking the baby into her arms. "Your niece."

"Oh." He paused before he answered. "Casie."

She noticed the hesitation. "You two aren't very close, are you?"

"No." He saw no reason to explain any more than he had to.

"So, Officer, now that I've changed your niece, what is it that I can do for you?"

Casie reached out to grab hold of the badge on his shirt. Liz watched in fascination as he took a step back. No, not close at all, she judged. What was he doing with the baby, then? It didn't make any sense.

He hated asking anyone for anything. Always had. He prided himself on being able to manage no matter what the situation. This, though, was different. Silently he cursed the guitar player for ever having wandered into his sister's life. "Sally, my sister, had to leave suddenly and I have to go to work, so..."

Explanations didn't come easily to him, Liz thought. "You'd like me to watch the baby?" she prompted. She had a spot in her heart for strays and lost puppies. Disgruntled and somber looking, the man qualified for the label.

He was relieved now that the words were out. "Yes. I'll pay you, of course."

Liz picked up a rattle and offered it to Casie. Casie eyed his badge one last time, then took the rattle. "That's usually the way it's done."

"Excuse me?"

Liz shook her head. Something wasn't quite right here. "I get the feeling that we're not quite in the same conversation. I'm usually reimbursed for watching children." She saw no lights going on as he took in this information. "You did come to me because I run a day care, didn't you?"

"Day care?"

For such a good-looking man, he certainly was slow-witted. A pity. "Day care," she repeated. "As in all those children you saw me with yesterday."

"They weren't yours?"

Liz stared at him incredulously. Casie gave up the rattle and began to chew on the front of Liz's jersey. "You thought they were all mine?"

"Well, yes." He saw the laughter in her eyes and felt instantly foolish. How was he to know that they weren't hers?

Liz laughed. "No wonder you looked at me so oddly yesterday."

Griff looked at his wristwatch. He should have been on his way already. "Um, it's getting late."

"Fine." She nodded as she pulled a corner of her jersey back from Casie. A big wet pattern was beginning to form across the front of her chest. It felt cold.

"We'll settle up when you come back tonight. Just leave me your name and a number where I can reach you."

He stopped, one foot already across the threshold. "Why?"

With her free hand, Liz picked up a large sketch pad and crayon from the coffee table. "In case of an emergency. Here."

He took the crayon from her and stared at it, puzzled. "What kind of an emergency?"

Liz shrugged. "You're a policeman. You should know better than me."

None of this was making any sense to him. The whole world had turned upside down in less than twenty-four hours. Maybe he could still locate his sister. With luck, she couldn't have gotten very far. Better yet, maybe he could locate that guitar player of hers. He wondered just how far the definition of justifiable homicide could be stretched in this case.

Griff began to write out his name and then stopped as the ludicrousness of the situation hit him. He held up his writing instrument.

"This is a yellow crayon."

"Yes, I know."

"You can hardly see the letters on the paper."

"That's all right, I can read it."

He frowned. Maybe he shouldn't be leaving his niece with this woman. The elevator was obviously not reaching the top floor. "Don't you have a pen?"

"Sure." Liz looked around, trying to remember where she had last seen one. "Somewhere. Want to wait?"

"No."

She gave him a broad smile. "Then you're stuck with a yellow crayon, I'm afraid."

With an impatient sigh, Griff hastily scribbled down the information she requested and then thrust the piece of drawing paper back into her hand. Without so much as a word to either of them, he beat a hasty retreat out the front door.

Liz looked down at the name. "Officer Griffin Foster," she read aloud, then looked at the closed door. She let the paper drop to the table and then turned her attention to the baby in her arms. The little girl made some sort of indiscernible noise by way of conversation.

"Yes, I know," Liz agreed.

She shifted Casie to her hip and then headed to her bedroom to get dressed. The other children would be arriving soon.

"I'm sorry to be the one to have to tell you this, Casie, but I'm afraid you have a very strange uncle."

Chapter Three

Liz looked at her watch. Six o'clock. She and Casie had now been together for almost twelve hours. All in all, it hadn't been a very trying experience. Casie had been the highlight of the day. The boys had all been excited about this newest member of their crowd. A little girl was a novelty at the day care and even Peter, who was eighteen months old, seemed to respond to the fact that something was different. As far as Liz could see, Casie seemed to have a very sweet disposition.

Not a thing like her uncle.

The children had all gone home now, disappearing from her life for all intents and purposes until seven-thirty Monday morning. All except this one, Liz thought as she stood over Casie who was sleeping on her bed. She had barricaded the bed with a semicircle of chairs to keep Casie from rolling off. Leaning over,

Liz tucked a light blanket around her. Casie went on sleeping.

Liz slipped out of the room and closed the door behind her.

Okay, so where was he? Granted, they hadn't established a specific pick-up time, but she had just naturally assumed that it would be this week, and more exactly, somewhere under twelve-and-a-half hours.

Liz stooped down to collect the pieces of a large puzzle that had not only been scattered, but chewed on. Did policemen abandon children? she wondered. Maybe, but she had a feeling that this one didn't. He wasn't in danger of winning away the title of Mr. Congeniality from anyone, but she'd bet that he was a straight arrow. Maybe too straight, she thought, remembering his unsmiling countenance. She mechanically placed the puzzle back into the large game box in the corner of the room, wondering if he ever loosened up a little.

Well, that wasn't her problem. Her problem was a certain small sleeping beauty who wasn't going to sleep indefinitely.

She decided to give him a little more time. Maybe there was a crime wave in progress and he was too busy to call. She grinned to herself as she straightened the coffee table where Nathan and Bruce had battled it out on opposite sides of "the castle." Crime wave. That would be a novelty. Nothing more serious ever happened in Bedford than a break-and-enter by bored, thrill-seeking teenagers.

She gave Griff until she finished straightening out the family room. The crayons were all back in their boxes, the toys stashed away in the toy box and the blank sheets of drawing paper were all stacked up, ready for a fresh set of eager hands on Monday. The room hadn't looked this neat in a long, long time.

Enough was enough.

She dug into the back pocket of her jeans and took out the carefully folded sheet with Griff's name and telephone number on it. What Officer Foster needed, she thought, was a gentle reminder. She had a life to get on with, too.

"Police station," a mildly irritated voice informed her. "Officer C.W. Linquist speaking."

"Is Officer Foster there, please?"

The pause on the other end of the line lasted so long Liz thought that the man hadn't heard her. She was about to repeat Griff's name when the other party came to life.

"Griff Foster?"

"Yes," she said a bit uncertainly. Was this some bizarre hoax? The man *was* a policeman, wasn't he? After all, he had stopped her yesterday. But if something wasn't wrong, why did the officer on the other end of the line sound so surprised?

"You want Officer Griffin Foster?"

"Yes." This time, her answer was a little more emphatic as well as impatient. She thought she heard a grin in the man's voice. "Is he there?"

"No, he's not. Are you registering a complaint?"

Liz thought she heard Casie begin to whimper. "Only that he's not there." She heard the man on the other end chuckle.

"You mean he has a date?"

"No, he has a niece. And he was supposed to have picked her up—earlier," Liz finally said for lack of a specific time to refer to. "Could you tell me where I could reach him?"

"Is this on the level? You want Griff Foster. Tall, dark brown hair, mustache—"

Yes, yes, Liz wanted to cry. "Speaks only when spoken to," she filled in.

"Yeah, that's Griff all right." There was noise in the background and he stopped to answer a question. "Sorry, things are a little hectic around here."

Welcome to the club, she thought. "So I gather," Liz said tightly. "Just where is the good officer now?"

"Home, I guess, where he is every night after work—or so he says."

Liz wasn't sure what the other man was implying and she didn't think she wanted to know. "Well, I need to reach him. He forgot a certain little bundle here, apparently."

"The sly dog."

"Does the sly dog have a phone number you could give me?"

"It's highly irregular," C.W. began.

Liz thought of herself as an infinitely patient person, but she had just about reached the end. "So is child abandonment."

"Just a minute," he said, and then recited the number. "But don't tell him you got it from me."

"The subject will never come up," she promised, then pressed the receiver button down, disconnecting them. She dialed the number C.W. had given her and after three rings heard a deep male voice respond.

Griff had hurried into the living room to pick up the phone. His keys were still in the door. Maybe it was Sally calling. "Yes?"

"Well, hello to you, too, Officer Foster. This is your conscience speaking."

"What?"

Obviously not up to jokes. She might have guessed. "You forgot to pick up something on your way home. Small, pink, wiggles and wets. Sound familiar?"

Griff closed his eyes. Damn, how could he have been so stupid? Because it was not part of his routine, picking up Casie had completely slipped his mind. But that was no excuse, he berated himself. "Oh, God."

"Ah, it all comes back to you now, does it?"

He didn't particularly care for this woman's sense of humor. He didn't particularly care for *any* of this. "I'll be right there."

"I should hope so." She heard a click in answer to her comment. "Certainly do run off at the mouth, don't you?" she murmured as she hung up.

Griff had put in a long and hard day. O'Hara, Ross, Henderson, Swayze and Brown had called in sick and that had left only a handful of officers to patrol the area. Then there had been that car accident off Main. The old man driving the boatlike Cadillac had suffered a heart attack and plowed right into a van whose driver was a young college student. Griff had been the first on the scene. The student was just badly shaken, but the old man was turning blue. A quick application of CPR had brought the man around, but he was in critical condition. Griff rode with him in the ambulance because the old man wouldn't let go of his hand. Griff had figured it was his duty to go along.

The old man had stayed on his mind the rest of the day, even when he was besieged from all sides by the avalanche of paperwork he had allowed to pile up. His attempts at locating Sally had proven fruitless. Lunch had been something small and greasy and three hours overdue that C.W. had tossed on his desk. He hadn't had a minute to call his own in the past twelve hours. By the time he had lowered himself behind the steering wheel of his car, a baby had been the last thing on his mind.

He wished he could pretend that it was all a bad dream, but he knew that it wasn't. He also knew that he couldn't figure out what he was going to do with his newly acquired niece. Sally had seemed to disappear without a trace. Someone on the radio was singing about how great life was. He switched it off.

Liz turned on the radio and caught the last few lines of a favorite song. She hummed along as she made herself a fresh pot of coffee. She loved listening to music. It seemed to somehow underscore life, make it more pleasant, highlight the good points and make the bad more bearable. She decided to leave the radio on as she waited for Griff to make his appearance. Listening to old familiar tunes would help ease the tension she felt building.

She wasn't sure why, but that big, solemn-looking policeman seemed to make her feel slightly tense when she was around him. Something about him made the hairs on the back of her neck stand on end.

Static, probably, she muttered, peeking into the bedroom. Casie was still fast asleep, curled up on her stomach and clutching the center of the comforter. Liz had just managed to ease the door closed when the doorbell rang.

He must live close by, she thought. Either that or he exceeded a lot of speed limits to get here. Somehow, she didn't think that was the case.

She opened the door and gave him her broadest smile. "Hi."

The smile was not returned. Griff did not like to be caught lacking. "I forgot her."

"I had a hunch."

He walked in. "I'm not used to remembering a baby."

"It's an acquired experience." She shut the door behind him. "Has your sister come back?"

Griff spun on his heel to face her and Liz could have sworn the look in his eyes was hostile. "What?"

Liz raised her hand, pretending to ward off his anger. She saw the look retreat. "You said she had to leave suddenly. I just wondered if she came back—suddenly."

"No."

"I see." The man was not going to win any awards as a great conversationalist. "Well, Casie's asleep on my bed if you want to get her." Liz began to lead the way toward the back of her house.

The baby grand that dominated the living room seemed to pique his interest. It was an heirloom and had once belonged to her grandmother, who gave recitals and smelled of vanilla. When she had moved away, she had insisted that her favorite grandchild take her most prized possession.

"Do you play?"

"Mostly children's songs," she admitted.

There was a photograph in a silver frame on top of the piano. It was of a subdued, handsome man in glasses, sporting a Vandyke. He looked cultured and refined, as if he'd be right at home at the opera. Griff took an instant dislike to him. He picked up the photograph and studied it.

"Husband?"

Liz turned around and saw him fingering Vinnie's photograph. "No."

He placed the frame back down carefully. "Boyfriend?" It was absolutely no concern of his if she had a harem, but he still heard himself asking.

Liz tried to picture her buddy Vinnie as her lover and almost laughed out loud. All she could think of was the way he had looked when she had rescued him from that sandlot bully when they were both eleven. She had won his undying devotion from that day forward. "Is this an investigation?"

"Just making small talk," Griff muttered uncomfortably, wondering why he was bothering to explain.

"Not very good at it, are you?"

He frowned. Served him right for asking. "If you'll just give me my niece."

He was obviously taking care of the child out of some sense of duty rather than love and it disturbed her. How could he not melt at the sight of that little girl? "Sounds as if you're ordering a ham on rye."

He almost told her what she could do with her analysis, but then, she had helped him out. "No, just a niece."

Liz paused at the bedroom door, her hand on the doorknob. "Have you eaten yet?"

What did that have to do with anything? "No."

Maybe that was it. She knew a lot of people who were churlish when they were really hungry. "Would you like to?"

He stared at her, not quite comprehending. "Are you asking me out?"

"No, I'm asking you in." She slipped her arm through his and nudged him toward the kitchen. "When we weren't playing with your niece, the boys and I made lasagna. There's more than enough to last me for at least the next week. I thought perhaps you'd like some."

He didn't want to get tangled up with this strange woman any more than he absolutely had to. Having Casie in his life was going to present enough problems. Liz was looking up at him with the same bright blue eyes his niece had. "No, I—"

He was being obstinate. Well, so could she. "We used real ingredients," she coaxed. "No mud or bugs."

She really was missing a few pieces to the final puzzle. "Is that what you do with them, cook?"

A male chauvinist if she ever saw one. "There's nothing wrong in teaching boys how to cook. And it makes them feel useful and it gives us an activity to share together." She grinned impishly. "Besides sliding through stop signs, of course."

No, he wasn't going to get involved here. "Thanks, but I'd better get home."

"All right. How about if I make you a care package?"

"A what?"

"A care package. I'll wrap up some lasagna for you to take home. You might get hungry later." She went to the pantry and took out a box of aluminum foil. "Unless your girlfriend objects to your bringing home food from strange women."

She had the last part right at any rate. "There isn't a girlfriend," he said before he realized it.

She had a feeling that there might not be. She also realized that his answer made her smile.

Griff hesitated. Oh well, what was the harm? He had eaten worse, he was sure—just this afternoon, as a matter of fact. "All right, if it's not too much trouble."

She took the pan out of the refrigerator and cut a rather large piece. "No trouble at all." Pulling up the sides of the foil, she secured Griff's dinner. After she put it in a paper bag, she found that, music in the background notwithstanding, she couldn't take the silence anymore. The man *did* only speak when spoken to. "I'm sorry about what I said earlier, about your not being very good at small talk."

Griff shrugged. "I'm not. It's not required in my line of work."

"Oh, I don't know." She deposited the bag on the kitchen table and looked up at him. Lord, he was tall. And masculine. Very, very masculine. Her probably had to put up one damn good fight to stay unattached. "I always thought policemen were the friendliest people in the world when I was a little girl. I think I was in love with the uniform."

Her eyes skimmed over him. He wasn't wearing his uniform now. He had on jeans, a turtleneck shirt that somehow made his throat all the more tempting to her, and a windbreaker that seemed a bit too light for the cool November weather. He probably didn't allow himself to get cold, she thought. Nevertheless, she thought she might try warming him up. "Would you like a cup of coffee?"

He wanted to go. Now. And yet, he didn't make a move. "No, I—"

"C'mon," she urged. "It's not poisoned." She was already pouring him a cup. "And besides, Casie's still asleep."

He watched her. Confident seemed to be the best word to describe her. "Doesn't anyone ever get to say 'no' to you?"

"Oh, they say it," she assured him, placing the mug in front of him, "but I don't listen."

"I noticed."

He knew he should be on his way home, away from this effervescent woman with the athletic body and overdeveloped sense of gab. But the thought of going home and being alone with Casie filled him with a sort of apprehension he wasn't familiar with. So he picked up the mug and held it in both hands.

She poured herself a mug and then sat down at the table. He remained standing. "You can sit down, you know. The chairs are pretty sturdy."

Awkwardly, he sat down.

Progress, Liz thought, of a sort. "Do you know how long your sister is going to be gone?"

The woman was impossible. Did she think she could delve into his life like this? "Does the word *privacy* mean anything to you?"

His tone didn't put her off. "Never got that far in the dictionary. I stopped at *n* for *neighborly*."

He reluctantly responded to the smile she gave him. "I don't know," he finally admitted. Griff took a long sip of his coffee.

"I see." The subject *was* painful to him. Liz knew enough to back off, even though she wanted to help somehow. "Would you like to bring Casie back on Monday—if your sister doesn't come back for her, I mean."

He nodded slowly. He didn't want to think about the possibility of Sally leaving Casie with him indefinitely, but it was becoming a very viable reality.

Because she knew that his sense of pride demanded it, Liz mentioned the financial end of the arrangement. "I could give you a weekly rate until the situation changes."

Griff reached into his back pocket for his checkbook. "How much do I owe you?"

Liz put out a hand to stop him. The sudden contact of bare skin on bare skin froze the moment, and they looked at each other. Liz wondered what was going on behind those eyes of his. Who was he? Why was he so remote? And who was this sister who abandoned her child on his doorstep? The part of her that longed to make everyone happy wanted to ask the questions aloud. But she kept her peace. She knew it was too soon for answers. "Why don't we take care of that next week?"

Her suggestion brought out a dry chuckle. "I've heard loan sharks use that line."

So you do have a sense of humor in there somewhere. That was promising. "Don't worry, I won't ask for any popular body parts in payment." She saw his eyebrows rise questioningly and realized that he must have misunderstood her. "Are you going to need any help in taking care of her over the weekend?" she asked quickly, eager to change the subject.

"No," he said automatically, then paused. "Yes."

"Is this a trick answer?"

Because it had been a long day, because a man had come back to life in his arms, Griff decided to allow himself a rare break in his own rules of keeping his own counsel. "I don't know when Sally is coming back and there are some things I guess I'll need to get for the ki—for Casie."

"Such as?"

"I don't know."

"That extensive, eh?"

Liz toyed with her coffee mug. This was really none of her business, but then, that had never stopped her before. Everything that came in contact with her life somehow turned out to be her business. "Would you like me to go shopping with you tomorrow?"

"Shopping?"

"For diapers, baby food, clothes, et cetera."

It was against his principles to ask for help, or to accept any. He had learned long ago to be self-sufficient. The only one he could depend on was himself.

"I don't like to ask for help."

"I would have never guessed." Her eyes danced as she said it. Her lips moved into a wide smile.

She had a mouth made for smiling. Would the smile spread to his own lips if he kissed her?

The thought was like cold water in his face. Griff took a deep breath, deciding that he was going ever so slightly insane because of overwork, the situation— and the woman. He put the mug down on the table and looked over his shoulder toward the bedroom.

"I think I might need help with the 'et cetera.'"

"That," she said, smiling over her coffee mug, "happens to be my specialty."

Chapter Four

Griff realized that he was squeezing his coffee mug. If it were possible to tranfer the tension he felt, he was certain that he'd probably be able to float a nickel on the surface of the dark liquid in his mug.

He had felt more relaxed drinking washed-out coffee from a foam cup while on a stakeout in the roughest neighborhoods of Los Angeles. He had worked in some of the seedier areas just before he had come to work in Bedford. On a stakeout he had always known what he was up against and how to react. He made sure he was in control.

Here, sitting in the brightly illuminated kitchen with cheery knickknacks abounding, he wasn't all that certain. Lack of certainty took precious control away from him. Granted, sharing a mug of coffee with an animated honey-blonde did not quite come under the heading of life or death. But then again, there was an undeniable degree of certainty in facing a life-or-death situation. If you lost your edge, if you got sloppy, you could quite possibly be blown away.

He had a strange, nagging suspicion that the same observation could be applied to this case if he looked at another meaning of being blown away: having the wind knocked out of him. The woman across from Griff made him feel that he was positively surrounded even though she remained sitting in her chair.

It was the way she looked at him when she talked, the way she sailed ahead, asking questions. She didn't seem to entertain the idea that perhaps she had no business asking the things she was asking.

And it was the way she gestured when she spoke. If she ever lost the ability to talk—an absolute godsend if it ever came to pass, he mused—she could still make herself understood. There were gestures and motions accompanying every sentence she uttered. And she uttered a hell of a lot of them.

Griff studied her thoughtfully over the rim of his mug, wondering just what it was that made him so wary around her. She was his exact opposite. Flamboyant, animated, bubbling over with enthusiasm. Yet that didn't put the edge into the situation. No, he dealt with exact opposites every day. Most people were not as reserved as he was. There was something more at work here. There was something about her that made him very, very nervous and he had a healthy respect for his own intuition.

Without quite knowing why, he felt that there was a very real danger of his being blown away by this very exceptional woman.

While she talked, Liz could feel his eyes on her, dissecting her. From the consternation on his face, she judged that he felt confused and not very pleased.

Liz nodded toward his mug. "Something wrong with the coffee?"

"No, why?"

"You're frowning over it. Or is it me that's making you look so cross?"

Enough. He had encountered less probing when he had interviewed to join the police force. He set his mug down. He thought he did it with finality. "It's been a long day, Ms. MacDougall—"

He thought wrong.

She was off and running with another topic. "Well, now, I've held your baby—"

"My *sister's* baby," he corrected tersely, and even that correction didn't make him happy. This baby had no place in his life, or Sally's.

Well, she wasn't in Sally's life right now, was she? She was in his.

Liz steamrolled over his protest as if she hadn't heard it. "Which automatically allows you to call me Liz." She drained her coffee. "Or Elizabeth if you prefer to be formal."

He thought longingly of tape, the large, heavy-duty kind used to wrap packages that were sent through the mail. Applying the wide tape in a strategic place might just bring a halt to her nonstop stream of words.

"Elizabeth," he began again, searching his soul for patience because she had come to his rescue when he needed it.

Liz nodded her head. She might have known. "You prefer to be formal. I had a hunch. I, of course, prefer to be informal." There was mischief in her eyes as she made the statement.

"I wouldn't have guessed." His sarcasm couldn't be held in check any longer.

She was impervious to his attempt to constrain her. His mouth was no match for hers and they both knew it. "Liz."

He stared, lost. Was she talking to herself now? He wouldn't doubt it. "What?"

"Call me Liz," she encouraged. "It's only one syllable and not very hard."

He sighed, placing his large hands flat on the table. "What apparently seems to be hard is making a getaway from here."

So why wasn't he getting up and leaving? It wasn't as if she had him tied to a chair, for heaven's sake. Yet he remained seated. He didn't quite know why.

Was this man really so eager to head for the hills? She was receiving some very contradictory signals from him. Verbally, he was saying that he couldn't wait to be away. But she was getting a distinctly different impression from his body language. Especially when his eyes washed over her.

"Oh, were you trying to leave?"

"Before the turn of the century, yes," he muttered darkly.

If his retort was meant to put her off, it failed. "Any wounded bears in your family?" She rose and took the two mugs to the sink.

"I have no family."

She turned to look at his expression. It warned her that she couldn't cross this barrier. She hesitated, considered, and then crossed, intrigued by the No Trespassing sign she perceived. "I take it your sister and Casie belong to the stork who brought them?"

He laughed despite himself. "Does anyone ever get to have the last word with you?"

She shut off the running water and put the mugs on the drainboard. Reaching for the kitchen towel to dry her hands, she grinned. "Nope."

"I didn't think so."

A plaintive, insistent cry emanated from Liz's bedroom.

She draped the dish towel on a magnetic hook hanging from the side of the refrigerator. "That would be your niece."

Time to go. Suddenly, a deep dread filled him. He didn't welcome the idea of staying home alone with the child. Weighing the two evils, if he were being honest with himself, Griff decided that despite the verbal barrage, staying with Liz was actually the less odious of the two. Almost eager to escape a moment ago, he hesitated now, casting about for a solution.

"How much is your weekend rate?"

Liz was about to lead the way to her bedroom. His inquiry, out of the blue, made her stop in her tracks. She looked at his face, trying to read what was going on behind that strong, impenetrable exterior. She thought she discerned a flash of apprehension in his eyes before the curtain went down again. He was probably one hell of a poker player. "I don't have a weekend rate."

The wail from the bedroom became more urgent. So did his thoughts. "Would you consider—"

Griff stopped. He was panicking. He had never done that, not in all his years on the force. Not since he was a child. What was the matter with him? Casie was, after all, only a six-month-old baby. Besides, he was sure that Sally would be coming back as soon as she fully realized what she had done. There was no reason to feel this apprehensive about the matter.

Liz could sense the feelings he was experiencing, or at least she thought she could. Her face softened and she smiled encouragingly at him. In a gesture meant to comfort, she put her hand on his shoulder.

"There's nothing to it, Griff. And you can call me anytime if you run into trouble."

She felt the muscle beneath her hand become rigid. Now what had she said wrong? she wondered in mounting exasperation. Here she was offering to help and he was acting as if she was about to embark on a crime spree. She couldn't decide whether he was just a clumsy, helpless male who was rather sweet and definitely out of his element, or a total neanderthal type whom she could wash her hands of completely.

But then, she knew she couldn't do that. She had never abandoned anything that needed help, not even that mean-spirited dog she had found on the way home from school when she was a child. In a way, Griff reminded her of that dog. The German shepherd hadn't trusted anyone either and it had taken a lot of patience, understanding and loving on her part before she finally brought the dog around. But once she had, he'd stayed with her for the duration of his life, giving her his undying loyalty.

A simple "thank you" would have sufficed here, she thought, then wondered how Griff would react to being compared to a dog. She had a hunch she knew. It made her grin again.

He didn't need pity or someone talking to him as if he were some bumbling idiot, although he grudgingly thought that the description might have fit in this instance.

"I can handle it from here. It'll be all right." Griff stood abruptly. The chair legs scraped against the kitchen floor as he backed up.

It sounded more like a command. "Plan to hold a gun on her if she doesn't follow orders?" Liz asked, her eyes dancing.

He couldn't decide if she was laughing at him or not, so he said nothing. Instead, he turned and walked to Liz's bedroom.

When he opened the door he saw that the room wasn't what he had expected. Somehow, he thought things would be scattered around, a testimony to the whirling dervish who normally slept there. Instead, the room, done in pale blues, grays and whites, echoed of softness, of womanliness. It made him acutely aware of the fact that he had been neglecting a very healthy, demanding part of himself.

Impatiently, he dismissed his thoughts.

Turning, he found her right behind him, so close that all he had to do was lean forward to kiss her. For a moment, he thought he was going to. In one unguarded moment he almost went with an impulse in-

stead of leading with his mind. Leading with his mind
had always been the safest route for him. Emotions,
yearnings, those were things to keep locked away.
They formed attachments and attachments formed
trouble. He couldn't get hurt if he left no openings in
the fence around him.

He struggled with himself and won.

She felt it, felt the tension, the electricity, perhaps
even the warring factions he was enduring. They certainly matched her own. She held her breath, her eyes
on his, willing him to make that first move. She found
that she was more than ready to meet him three quarters of the way, but that first move had to be his.

He turned away and she wanted to kick him for
being a coward. There could be no other reason he
hadn't kissed her. She had seen the desire flare in his
eyes, had felt his gaze hot and wanting on her face.
Why hadn't he followed through? What was he afraid
of?

Well, there was a baby to see to, so her own needs
had to go on hold. "You want me to check her out
before you take her?" She came up beside him.

He wasn't following her again. Damn it, why didn't
the woman talk straight? "Check her out?"

Casie was waving her hands about. Liz took one of
them and curled her fingers around it. Casie gurgled
in recognition.

"To see if she's wet. Or would you rather do the
honors yourself?" Liz raised her brow questioningly,
barely hiding her amusement.

Griff took a step back from the chair-surrounded bed, as if to give her room. "No, that's okay, you go right ahead."

"You're all heart." She reached for a diaper from the pile on the nightstand. "It's made of stone, but you're all heart."

"How would you know what my heart's made of?" he demanded, his voice dangerously low.

He shouldn't have even bothered answering her, he told himself. Yet he had. Why was he allowing this woman to get under his skin this way?

She deposited the wet diaper into the blue diaper pail, and glanced over her shoulder. "Then why didn't you kiss me just before?" The question exploded from her lips.

Nice going, Liz. You really know how to play hard to get.

Well, she had gone this far, no use leaving the rest dangling in the air. "You wanted to." Expertly, she tucked the baby's bottom onto the new diaper and secured it.

If ever a woman deserved the label "impossible," it was the one before him. "I also wanted to strangle you a minute ago, but I didn't do that, either."

"Murder's against the law." She smoothed own Casie's dress. "Kissing isn't."

In a duel of words, he knew he was outmatched. The past half hour had taught him that. Still, he didn't back off. "Maybe it's against mine."

"Laws are made to protect people."

"Exactly."

She turned, a challenge in her eyes. "Are you afraid of me?"

He should have just ignored her, should have just taken his niece and driven away. Instead, he met her challenge head-on. He had done smarter things in his time.

Afterward, when he tried to explore his reasons, he wasn't sure why he had done it, why he had walked into the lion's den and exposed himself to the danger that lurked within. Maybe it was to show her that he wasn't afraid. Maybe it was to show himself. Maybe it was just to silence her for a moment. More than likely it was because he really wanted to, because the question of what it would be like to kiss her had lingered in the back of his mind ever since she had winked at him yesterday afternoon.

And when he could think, he also realized that his earlier assessment about being blown away had been very, very accurate.

The kiss had not been gentle. There had been anger in it, then passion and wonder had begun turning around in his head like a fiery kaleidoscope that temporarily removed him from the real world. He had meant to silence her. He had never meant to wound himself.

But he did.

There was a laugh on Liz's lips when he began to kiss her. It vanished as his unbridled desire, naked and raw, surged up to meet her. Kissing Griff was like being sucked into the center of a tornado. There had been no time for her to prepare for what was happening, no time for her to build up to this. No way of knowing that there were going to be bombs bursting in air.

His kiss ripped her away from her bedroom and transported her to Oz in one mind-blinding flash. Anchoring herself by putting her hands on his arms, she rose up on her toes, letting herself go, letting herself fall into the swirling abyss that he created for her.

Hungers rose, full-bodied and demanding, within Griff. He cupped the back of her head with his hand, tipping her face up toward his and his kiss ravaged her and devastated him. Over and over, his lips met hers. The assault was merciless and yet he wasn't the master here. Something else was. And that something scared the hell out of him. Sweet as her mouth was, he forced himself to pull away before there was nothing left of him.

Reality slowly came into focus. In an effort to pull herself together, Liz pressed her hands against Griff's chest. To her pleasure, the beating of his heart was erratic. Her own heart had just broken the sound barrier.

"Maybe I'm the one who should be afraid," she whispered, her voice unsteady, her pulses refusing to subside to a normal rhythm.

He looked down into her face, the temptation to kiss her again, to make love to her, almost too great to resist. Which was exactly why he had to. No ties. No binds. Not on him.

"Maybe."

As if she had been ignored long enough, Casie sent up a protest. Stepping away from one another almost awkwardly, they turned toward the baby on the bed.

Liz tickled the baby's tummy. Tiny booted feet kicked in pleasure. "I think she was jealous."

"There's nothing to be jealous of," he retorted a bit too quickly.

"We'll work on it," she promised with a wink.

The kiss they had shared had opened up channels and raised more questions for Liz than it had answered. One thing she was certain of, this was not a passionless man. Just one, she sensed, who had been hurt by something or someone and now was bound and determined that it wouldn't happen again.

She had no intention of hurting him. But she *was* going to get close. He intrigued her too much for her to turn away now.

Taking a deep breath to calm herself, Liz picked Casie up and handed the squirming baby to Griff. "Here."

He held his arms out and accepted the infant as if he had been passed a sack of grain.

"No, no, no." Liz shook her head. "It's a baby, not a bomb, Griff."

"A lot you know," he muttered.

"Yes, I do," she agreed.

He had a sinking feeling that she was going to begin expounding upon the topic right then and there. Instead, she took the baby back. Had she changed her mind about keeping Casie overnight?

His hopes died when she held Casie out to him again. "Now take her into your arms the way you would something precious." His hold on the small child was just as stiff as before. "Did you ever have a pet kitten?"

"No."

She hadn't expected a negative answer. She had had four cats. And three dogs. She tried again. "A puppy?"

"No."

Liz cocked her head, studying him in wonder. "Didn't you have any pets?"

"What does that have to do with it?" he asked impatiently.

"A lot, I'm beginning to think." Her expression had grown serious. Maybe he'd never had to take care of anything before. In that case, she'd have to go slower. "Touching is part of bonding."

"I don't want to bond, I just want to take her home."

That last part wasn't exactly true, but she was his responsibility for the time being and he refused to shirk his responsibilities. He looked around the room. "Where's her chair?"

"You mean her infant seat?"

He nodded shortly. "Whatever."

"In the living room." Shaking her head, she led the way out. He was going to take more time than her German shepherd had, she decided. She pointed to the seat on the floor. "Want to carry her in that?"

"Yes."

She picked it up and put it on the coffee table. "You're shutting yourself off from a great opportunity."

"My loss," he muttered sarcastically as he strapped the baby in.

"Yes, it is," she said quietly.

He shot her a silencing look and Liz stepped back, hands raised in temporary surrender. She looked on quietly as Griff hefted the baby seat up into his arms. He appeared more comfortable now that there was a barrier between him and his niece.

Why? Were relationships so painful to him? She refused to believe he was just a selfish, ungiving man. That kiss had made her feel otherwise. And there was something in his eyes that told her he had lived through a lot of pain. You had to be able to feel in order to be subjected to pain. There was a sensitive man in there somewhere and she was going to bring him out.

"Well," Griff muttered, "thanks." He turned and moved toward the front door.

Liz followed him. As an afterthought, she grabbed one of her cards that she had left on the hall table. Because there was no other available opening, she tucked the card into his back pocket. "Here."

He turned around, acutely aware that she had brushed her hand against his posterior. It had been done in innocence, but it had still happened. And he felt himself reacting to it and to her again. He had to get out. She was playing tricks on his mind and on his body, however unintentionally—and he was beginning to have his doubts about the latter being totally true.

"What do you think you're doing?"

"I'm giving you my card, of course. It has my home number on it in case you find that you have any questions—about the baby, I mean."

"Why else would I call?"

Liz opened the door for him. "Think about it." She leaned against the doorjamb as Griff crossed over the threshold. He did seem quite eager to get away, she thought.

She smiled down at the baby. "Don't be too hard on him, Casie. I have a feeling he'll get the hang of it eventually."

"There isn't going to be an eventually." He'd find Sally if he had to turn all of Southern California upside down.

"Whatever you say."

He glared at Liz. It was evident from her tone that she was humoring him.

She called after him as he started to leave. "Ten a.m.'s a good time."

"For what?"

"To pick me up. Shopping. Baby clothes, remember?" She put her hands on her hips, feigning exasperation. "Officer Foster, do they give memory courses down at the precinct?"

"No, they don't have SWAT training, either. I'll bring it up at the next meeting." He turned and walked to his car, holding the infant seat against his chest.

"Have a nice night."

She had no idea what it was that he mumbled back at her, but she thought it wiser not to ask.

Chapter Five

All he wanted to do was to get some sleep. He didn't think, after the long, arduous day he had put in, that it was too much to ask.

Obviously it was.

Both his mind and his new, uninvited house guest conspired against him. The latter's loud, demanding cries arrived like clockwork. Uncannily, they echoed through the otherwise quiet house each time that he finally found a comfortable position for himself and started to drift off to sleep.

As he trudged into Sally's old bedroom for the fifth time in as many hours, Griff looked down accusingly at the small, puckered face.

"Don't you ever sleep, kid?"

Normally, all protests ceased at the sound of the words. Her eyes would open wide at the different, low voice. The previous four wailing bouts had all been entreaties for attention, except for the one time she had gotten her body mysteriously tangled up in the dark comforter. This time, she just continued crying. She had kicked off her covers and her problem became obvious once Griff took a closer look at her.

Casie was wet, very, very wet and miserable. He stood contemplating what lay ahead of him and he didn't like it, but there was no way out.

Like it or not, he was going to have to change her diaper.

"No way that you can hang on until morning, is there, kid?"

Casie's answer was to wail louder. For such a small thing, her cries were exceptionally lusty and full.

Griff shook his head. He knew when he had lost a battle. With a resigned sigh, he reached down to where he had dropped Sally's oversize purse. Rummaging around, he pulled out one of the last remaining diapers.

What if it wasn't just a wet diaper? What then?

He didn't want to think about that. He was having enough trouble dealing with having to change her at all. When Liz had done the honors, she had made it seem so simple. Maybe for her, but not for him.

He stared down at the plastic rectangle in his hand, wondering how he had come to this moment in his life. He was a man who wasn't afraid to get his hands dirty. He'd dug ditches in his time, sweat and grime mixing and embedding themselves in his hands. He'd rather face a full day digging in the mud than three minutes of peeling back a dirty diaper.

He had no choice. She wasn't going to stop wailing until he changed her. Besides, if he left the wet diaper on her long enough, she'd probably come down with some kind of rash. He didn't want her in his life, but he didn't want her to suffer, either. And if Casie suffered, Griff knew full well that he would, too.

Especially his ears.

Taking a deep breath, he looked around for a way to open the diaper. Casie began to squirm.

"Hold still. This isn't fun for me, either," he grumbled as he pulled at the two plastic tabs on either side of the rounded tummy. The tabs didn't come off easily. Tugging, he wound up removing pieces of the accompanying plastic and inner cotton as well. The latter was decidedly soggy.

Not a very good first attempt, he thought in annoyance, throwing the pieces down on the carpet. He wondered how many more times he'd have to go through this ordeal before he found Sally.

Gingerly, he lifted back the diaper and then frowned. For a moment, he contemplated just closing it all up and returning to his room. Damn, he hadn't asked for this. He had no idea how to go about cleaning her up.

Yes, he did. That was just the trouble. Swearing under his breath softly enough so that Casie couldn't hear the words, he reached for a diaper wipe and began.

Casie wound up needing extensive cleaning. By the time Griff was finished, so was the towel he had dragged out of the bathroom.

"How can something so little be so dirty?" Griff marveled as he looked down at his niece.

Casie had only a pleased smile in answer to his question.

"Proud of yourself, aren't you? Well, don't be. I would have done it for anyone." He paused, the baby's wide blue eyes holding his own. "Okay, maybe not just anyone. Now get to sleep."

He pulled the covers over her again. The heap that had accumulated on the floor was something he'd contemplate tomorrow. It wasn't going anywhere. And neither would he if he didn't get some sleep.

He saw her following him with her eyes. Just as he reached the door and began to slip out of the room, Casie began to cry again.

"Now what?" he demanded, his hand braced on the doorjamb.

Because she had no way of answering, and because she went on crying, he marched back into the room. She looked so unhappy and forlorn that he found himself picking her up without thinking. He had forgotten that he wanted as little physical contact with her as possible. As he sat down, he cradled her against his chest.

Casie stopped crying.

"Is this what you wanted?" He held her up so that their faces were close to each other. Casie looked as if she was smiling in satisfaction. "God, six months old and a manipulator already. You're going to make one heck of a woman—like someone else I know." He thought of Liz and made himself push the image out of his mind.

Casie drooled in reply and patted one tiny hand on the fine covering of hair on his chest.

He didn't want to feel what he was feeling when he held her in his arms. Long-ago emotions stirred within him, spreading faster than the warmth on his chest created by the heat of her small hand. There was a bittersweet ache going through him.

Softly, he began to sing to Casie. It was a song he used to sing to Sally when they were alone together at night, to keep her from being afraid. Somehow, it seemed the natural thing to do.

After several minutes, Casie's even breathing told him that she had fallen asleep.

"Your mother used to react to my singing the same way," he whispered.

He raised her small body up over the barricade of chairs and slowly he lowered her to the bed, holding his breath. Casie went on sleeping.

Griff tiptoed out, hoping that he could finally get some rest. With any luck, Casie would sleep for the rest of the night. There were only a couple of hours left until morning, anyway.

Casie might sleep, but he discovered that he certainly couldn't. Every time Griff began to drift off to sleep, *she* came into his mind. Liz, with her laughing blue eyes and her mouth that was made for kissing—when it wasn't moving faster than the speed of light.

Damn her!

In exhausted disgust, Griff sat up in bed, running his hands through the mop of dark hair that fell into his eyes. He didn't deserve this, didn't deserve to be mentally battered by two females at the same time.

The only female who had ever mattered to him was still out there somewhere, running from herself and from him.

And here he was stuck with his niece and a very odd baby-sitter.

But while he could temporarily banish one from his mind because she was finally sleeping soundly, he had no such luck with the other. The way Liz's mouth had felt against his in that unexpected kiss kept replaying itself in his mind. As he involuntarily relived it, his body took over, aching for things that were only too normal. Turning against him and tormenting him with longings he had no intention of fulfilling.

He had half a mind to tell Liz that he didn't need her help with his niece any longer. He could take it from here. He had diapered Casie, hadn't he? And they had both survived, right? They'd both survive everything else that came their way, as well.

Oh, God, he was thinking of the two of them as a unit already. They weren't a unit, he insisted to himself. Casie was just Sally's little girl and he was stuck taking care of her until his sister turned up.

As for the other one... Griff threw himself down on his pillow, swearing.

"You look terrible."

"Thanks." Griff marched into Liz's living room, Casie tucked under his arm like a football.

Well, at least he was more casual about holding the baby, Liz observed.

She shut the front door, then turned to talk to the baby. "Hi, Puddin'." She took Casie from him and

effortlessly gathered her against her hip while holding
her with one arm. "Didn't she let you sleep?"

There was something natural about the way she
looked with a baby on her hip like that. Something
warm and maternal. Something he had never experi-
enced except vicariously when he was very young.
Something he had once longed for.

Griff dismissed the thought from his mind and the
feelings that surfaced with it. They had no place in his
well-ordered life. At least it had been well-ordered
until a couple of days ago.

"About an hour and a half."

"I told you to take it easy on him," Liz cooed to
Casie. The baby laughed.

"Well, you two just go ahead and share a laugh over
it," Griff muttered.

He really did look rather adorable with just a hint
of stubble on his face and that tired, droopy look
around his eyes. Even his mustache looked tired.
"Want some coffee before we get started?"

He considered her offer longer than she thought it
warranted. It wasn't that hard a decision.

"That depends."

"On what?" Liz pulled back her T-shirt from
Casie's grasp.

"On whether conversation goes with it."

Griff turned in Liz's direction only to see the firm
outline of her breasts beneath the bright pink cotton
T-shirt as Casie yanked on it, pulling it taut. Despite
the fact that he was bone tired, desire licked at him,
making him want her.

Damn, why didn't the woman wear a bra? For that matter, didn't she own a skirt? A long skirt that covered up her legs? The shorts she had on left little to his imagination and yet fired it up a good deal. It was winter. Didn't she know she wasn't supposed to wear shorts anymore? Never mind that the days were unseasonably warm lately.

He looked positively fierce. Did her talking bother him that much? Why? she wondered. "What's your preference?"

Lady, right now you wouldn't want to know what my preference is. "Guess."

From the look on his face, Liz had no trouble arriving at a conclusion. She pointed toward the kitchen. "Coffee's in there. Help yourself."

The coffee didn't help. Nothing, he thought, would help, short of a good nap. That, and maybe a long, cold shower. One had nothing to do with the other. Two days with Casie in his life and already it was turned upside down.

He rinsed his cup in the sink. Liz was playing with Casie at the table. He took her arm and helped her up from her chair. His manner wasn't altogether gentle.

"C'mon, let's go and get this thing over with," he growled.

The man needed a personality transplant. She hurried to keep up with his long stride and barely had time to close the front door behind her.

"We're going shopping, Foster, not to the dentist." She placed Casie in the car seat that Griff had installed in the back seat and strapped her in.

"Same thing," he muttered, then turned in time to be confronted with a very tempting view of her posterior as she bent over to accomplish her task.

Yup, he figured, the shorts were much too short. And her legs were much too long. Why couldn't she have stubby piano legs instead of long slim ones that made him wonder what it would be like to slide his hands along the smooth, tanned skin?

He jammed his hands into his pockets as he circled the car to the driver's side.

She bounced into the passenger side. "Are you always this pleasant first thing in the morning?"

"I didn't have a morning," he told her as he got in. "Just one endless night." He started up the car, then realized that he hadn't the faintest idea where they were going. "Where to?"

Liz reached around and buckled her seat belt. "I thought perhaps we'd hit the South Coast Plaza Mall for her clothes and crib, unless you—"

"Whoa, hold on, lady." He held up one authoritative hand. "What crib?"

"The crib she's going to be sleeping in," Liz answered simply. What was his problem? "She has to sleep somewhere, Foster."

"She is sleeping somewhere. She's sleeping on Sally's bed."

"Where she could easily roll off and hurt herself," she pointed out patiently.

"I've barricaded the perimeter just the way you did." He waited. Her expression didn't change. "I'm not going to buy her a crib. This isn't going to be a permanent arrangement."

Liz pushed the sleeves of her cardigan up to her elbows. "So then you've heard from your sister?"

He realized that he was pressing down too hard on the gas pedal and eased up. Why did he let her get to him this way? "Why do you have the habit of asking questions I don't want to answer?"

"I'd say that would cover just about everything except whether or not it was raining—and I'm not overly certain about that."

Maybe she was right. Maybe he was being too hard on her. "The weather's an open subject."

His solemn expression hadn't changed, but his tone softened. "Ah, progress." She turned in her seat to look at him. "Look, Griff, I'm only trying to help you."

Are you? he wondered. Then why are you preying on my mind the way you are? People who help don't mess up other people's minds. He was just overly tired, he told himself. And she was an attractive woman. But he had seen attractive women before. None, of course, whose mouths could be categorized as deadly weapons under two very separate, distinct headings.

"Yeah." He relented. "I know."

"Then act like it, for heaven's sake. Believe it or not, there could be other things I could be doing than going shopping for baby things."

He knew she was right and that he should be grateful for the help. But expressing gratitude came hard to him. "Sorry."

She grinned. "Is that a first for you?"

"Is what a first for me?"

"Apologizing."

He remembered the way his father had made him apologize for everything, for the very fact that he even existed. "No." His voice rang hollow.

This time she didn't comment on his response. Instinct told her not to. There was something dark and hurting there that he didn't want touched. It made her want to soothe it, to help. She had no idea why she wanted to get close to him, but she did. It wasn't physical attraction alone, although Lord knows, she'd never before kissed a man who made bombs burst in midair for her. But it went beyond that, way beyond the physical. Maybe she was being foolish, but she felt he *needed* her. And she was a sucker for that.

"We could get a portacrib," Liz volunteered abruptly as they turned off the freeway.

Her statement, out of the blue, threw him. He told himself he should be getting used to that. She seemed to carry on several different conversations at the same time. "What's that?" He pulled his car into the underground parking structure.

"It's a kind of traveling playpen with a thin mattress so that she can sleep in it as well as play in it." She went on talking as he got out and circled the front of the car. "I wouldn't recommend one to be used for a permanent sleeping arrangement, but it'll do in a pinch."

He opened the door for her, but made no move to unstrap Casie. "Is it comfortable?"

Liz got out and did the honors for Casie. Rather than wait to see if he'd pick her up, she took the baby into her arms herself. She looked at Griff with wide-eyed innocence.

"Why should sleeping on a board with a paper-thin mattress not be comfortable?"

Without thinking, Griff took Liz's arm to guide her out as cars came whizzing into the parking structure. "I'll buy a crib. No reason she shouldn't be comfortable." And maybe Sally would stay once she came back, he added silently. Then she'd need a crib for the baby.

Liz smiled to herself. She knew she hadn't been wrong about him.

Griff found that he could go through an incredibly large amount of money in an incredibly short amount of time with Liz at his side. Casie had next to nothing when they entered the mall, except for what was in his sister's purse. That could no longer be said, he thought as he signed yet another charge slip, this time for a white canopied crib and matching dresser.

"You sure the mall isn't giving you a kickback for all this?" Griff pocketed his charge card. "This card has seen more action in the last two hours than in the four years that I've had it."

"It's easy once you get the hang of it." Liz laughed. "And I'm not the one who decided to buy a play out-fit for your niece in every color."

"They were on sale."

"Right."

She was pleased with the way things had gone this morning. Griff was proving her right despite himself. Though he grumbled and muttered each time he paid for something, the love Griff was trying to deny that he had for his niece kept surfacing in different ways.

He watched Liz shift beneath the burden of the sleeping child in her arms as she tried to keep up with him. "She too heavy for you?"

"She seems to have gained a few pounds in the last couple of hours." Her arms were beginning to feel numb, but she wasn't about to ask Griff for help. That had to come from him.

With a resigned sigh, he took the sleeping baby from her. With more ease than before, he laid the small head against his shoulder. Liz looked surprised at his action, but for once, mercifully, said nothing about it.

"What's next?" he asked.

"A carriage might come in handy. A small, temporary one," she couldn't resist adding.

"If your day-care center ever folds, you can always get a job as a stand-up comedienne." He gestured with his free hand. "Lead on."

They took the escalator down to the ground floor of the mall. In the center was a large, shiny carousel. A long line of impatient children and slightly wilted parents circled halfway around it as they waited for their turn on the gaily colored horses.

Griff glanced at Liz as they stepped off the escalator. "No way. I am not waiting in line for thirty minutes so that she can ride around for two."

Liz grinned. "I wasn't going to ask. She's a little young, anyway."

"Just so you know," he muttered.

Just as they passed the carousel to enter a store that specialized in children's furnishings, Griff heard his name being called.

"Griff? Griff Foster?"

C.W. and Ernie approached him, looking wary, as if they were expecting to be proven wrong at the very last minute.

"Hey, man, it *is* you," C.W. cried. He stood on one side of Griff as Ernie flanked Liz.

Ernie eyed Liz and it was plain to Griff that there was nothing short of appreciative hunger in the older man's eyes. Griff found himself edging closer to Liz and putting his body between the two of them.

"Yeah, it's me." He seemed loath to say anything else.

Liz took the bull by the horns. She extended her hand to C.W. since he was the closer of the two. "Hi, I'm Liz MacDougall."

C.W. took her hand in his with no hesitation. "I'm C. W. Linquist."

"Ernie Brewster." Ernie lost no time in edging C.W. out of the way and taking Liz's hand himself. "I work very closely with Griff." He looked over toward Griff, who was scowling. "Well, maybe not that closely." He gave Liz a broad smile.

"Hey, Griff, I like your lady." C.W. gave him a nudge with his elbow.

Griff didn't need C.W.'s approval or any of the talk in the locker room he knew he was in for. "She's not my lady."

Of course she wasn't, but the way he denied it so vehemently stung. The intensity of her reaction to his words surprised her. She forced a smile. "I'm just a friend," Liz clarified.

"Didn't know you had any of those, Griff. No offense," Ernie added hurriedly. Ernie's expression did not go unnoticed by Griff. The man's eyes skimmed over Liz's legs again as if he were drinking them in for some future fantasy.

"Now you know." Griff took Liz by the arm and guided her away without bothering to say goodbye.

"See you in the precinct on Monday," C.W. said after Griff's retreating back. There was a chuckle evident in his voice.

"Nice meeting you both," Liz called to them over her shoulder.

"Do you have to wear shorts that—that short?" Griff grumbled harshly into her ear. "Don't you know it's winter? You're supposed to wear pants."

His breath felt warm against her ear and it tingled inside her. But she wasn't going to be intimidated by his voice. She had a feeling he wouldn't respect anyone who wouldn't go toe-to-toe with him. And anything less wasn't her style.

"Winter in Southern California doesn't count when the thermometer hits seventy-five. Besides, you didn't complain about my shorts before. Are you jealous?" she asked, recalling the way Ernie had ogled her.

"Why the hell should I be jealous of them? I'm just not interested in starting any riots. I'm a policeman, remember?"

She rose on her toes and kissed his cheek just before they entered the baby store. "You're lying, Griff Foster. I can see right through you."

"For your sake," he told her as he followed her into the store, "I hope that isn't true."

His justifiable homicide list was expanding by leaps and bounds.

Chapter Six

Liz rushed into her house, dropped her purse on the sofa and glanced at the clock on the mantel. Seven o'clock. Only thirty minutes to get ready.

It was her own fault. She knew she should have left Griff's house long before she did but with each attempt to leave, a new excuse seemed to crop up to make her stay for just a few more minutes. A few minutes had networked themselves into three hours. Somehow, she just couldn't manage to tear herself away from Casie. Or from Griff. How could she have left someone who was so hopelessly inept when it came to dealing with the baby's needs? To do so would have been displaying behavior bordering on cruelty. She felt compelled to give him at least some basic pointers.

Besides, for reasons she hadn't totally sorted out yet, she really liked being with him.

When she had made a comment that afternoon about how adorably hopeless he was, he had indignantly informed her that he had changed Casie during the previous night. It had taken a lot for Liz not to laugh out loud as she had tried to envision Griff tackling a diaper. She had far more success envisioning him tackling an escaping felon. He was undoubtedly a lot better at that.

The image of him struggling to diaper Casie's wiggling bottom brought a smile to her lips even as she rifled through the dresses in her closet, searching for one to wear to the concert. Her old standby would do fine, she decided offhandedly, her mind still on Griff. There was something very endearing about seeing such a big, strapping man looking so lost.

"Speaking of lost," she murmured to herself, "where's my other shoe?"

She moved several pairs of shoes around, searching through the bottom of her closet. She didn't have time to play hide-and-seek with an errant shoe. From the condition of her closet floor, it looked as though Alec and Bruce had used this one as one of their battlefields while she had been busy feeding Casie yesterday.

The shoe turned up under her bed.

She glanced at her wristwatch. The only way she was going to make it on time was if Vinnie was fifteen minutes late. Knowing Vinnie the way she did, this was not too much to hope for.

Laying her things out on the bed, Liz looked longingly toward the bathtub. Earlier, she had promised herself a long, luxurious bubble bath. A shower would have to do now. A very quick shower at that. But the trade-off had been well worth it. Every minute she had spent with Casie and Griff had been nothing short of an exciting adventure that left her amused, exasperated and more than a little entertained. Griff was responsible for most of that. And he was to blame for all the emotions that were rioting through her now. There were no two ways about it. The man had her emotions in an utter state of chaos. The message Don't Tread on Me was posted like a banner across his chest, and yet there was something in his eyes that reached out to her. Which was the true signal? She wasn't altogether sure, but she was bound and determined to find out.

Twenty-three minutes later, she stood showered, dried and dressed. She looked herself over in the mirrored wardrobe door. The dress she wore was a soft rose affair with narrow straps, a low neckline and shimmery beadwork woven throughout, like so many whimsically blinking stars. It fit snugly against her and was slit high up the front for maximum ease of movement. The light from her bedroom lamp played on the beadwork, making it glisten and shine. It was an ethereal effect that made her feel dreamy and exceptionally feminine.

She wished that Griff could see her in it.

"Might just make him sit up and take notice." She worked pins strategically into her hair.

She slipped on one shoe and was just reaching for the other when the doorbell rang.

Why did Vinnie have to pick tonight to start a new precedent and be on time? She still had her makeup to do and wanted at least five minutes to catch her breath.

Maybe it wasn't Vinnie.

Hobbling, Liz moved quickly to the front door, one shoe still in her hand. She yanked the door open. A part of her, a rather large part, was hoping that it was Griff coming to see her on some pretext about the baby. She knew he would never admit to wanting to see her on his own. For some reason, that would be admitting too much.

But the thin, bearded young man dressed in a tux was definitely not Griff. He lacked about six inches in the shoulder girth, let alone in height.

She kept her smile in place, trying to hide the disappointment that had absolutely no place being there. "Oh, hi, Vinnie, come on in. I'm almost ready." She closed the door behind him.

Vinnie glanced down at her one bare foot. "So I see." He strolled into the living room and fastidiously moved his photograph several inches to the left on the piano.

Liz hurried back toward her bedroom to apply some last-minute makeup.

Vinnie looked over in her direction. "You know, I'm really disappointed, Liz."

Liz spared him a glance before disappearing into the room. "Why?"

"This is probably the first time in my life that I'm on time, and you don't seem to appreciate it."

"I appreciate everything about you, Vinnie," she called out to him.

Bracing one hand on the bureau, she slipped on her shoe. One quick check in the mirror told her that mascara wouldn't really be missed just this once. Two strokes of her lip gloss and she was ready.

She came out of her bedroom to find Vinnie frowning to himself.

"Wish I could find a woman to say that."

"Say what?" With practiced hands, Liz straightened his bow tie.

Vinnie kept his chin raised as she worked. "That she appreciated everything about me."

Throwing a thin wrap about her shoulders, she hoped the evening wouldn't turn too cold. "I just did."

Vinnie looked wistful. "I mean a real woman—"

She patted his cheek. "Keep going, Vinnie, you've still got one foot left to go."

Vinnie looked at her, the myopic eyes behind the large-rimmed glasses suddenly appearing to focus on her and the impact of his words. "I meant one who isn't my best friend."

She was used to Vinnie's tongue getting hopelessly entangled. How he managed to turn out succinct, cryptic theater reviews for the local paper was one of life's little mysteries. "Nice save, Vinnie."

"Say." Vinnie stopped rambling long enough to look at her closely. "You look a little flushed."

Automatically, she raised her hand to her cheek. She *felt* a little flushed. But getting ready for the concert was only the superficial reason. She glossed over it. "That comes from rushing around. Let's go or we'll be more than fashionably late."

She dragged him by the arm to the front door. Though he acquiesced physically, he didn't seem ready to let the subject drop.

He peered at her face. "Are you coming down with something?"

The door clicked shut behind them, and they headed toward his car. She thought of the churning sensations in the pit of her stomach that had been there ever since Griff had kissed her. "Maybe."

"If you don't feel well, I can always go alone." In an instant, his face fell and he looked like a woeful child who had just been informed that his trip to Disneyland was canceled. Vinnie pushed his sliding glasses up on the bridge of his nose. "It won't be the first time I've gone by myself to review a concert."

He did have a flair for the dramatic, she thought. A painful flair. "Oh, Vinnie, don't sound so mournful." She opened the door to his gray sedan. "I'll go with you. I have nothing that's contagious." Unfortunately. Griff certainly hadn't acted as if he had been afflicted the way she was.

Vinnie got in next to her on the driver's side, but he was still apparently unsatisfied with her answer. "Then it's nothing serious?"

"The ignition, Vinnie. Put the key into the ignition." She watched him jab the key in, jiggle it and then turn on the engine.

Was it serious? she mused to herself. She didn't know yet. Aloud, she said, "That, only time will tell."

Vinnie began to drive toward The Performing Arts Center. "Have you seen a doctor?"

She smiled. Maybe she should. Someone who'd examine her head. Officer Griffin Foster gave her the impression, at times, that he was going into this relationship kicking and screaming. And that if he had his druthers, there wasn't going to *be* any sort of a personal relationship. So why was she bent on beating her head against the wall? Why did she want to be involved with a man who had to be cajoled into smiling?

"They haven't invented a serum for this yet, I'm afraid."

Vinnie swallowed. His voice dropped to a hoarse whisper. "Is it—is it inoperable?"

She realized that he was genuinely concerned and that they were talking about two very different things. She laughed softly, putting her hand on his arm. "Only if they cut out my heart." He stared at her, obviously utterly confused. "Vinnie, Vinnie," she said with great affection, "I think I'm falling in love, or like, or something in that family."

He let out a long, loud sigh. Behind him, car horns sounded impatiently.

"The light's green," Liz prompted.

The car began to move again. "You had me scared to death, Liz."

She nodded and grew serious for a moment. What would the consequences be if she did let herself fall in love with Griff? *Let.* Did she really have that much of a choice in the matter? She wasn't all that sure that she did, and that was what frightened her—in a thrilling, exhilarating sort of way.

"Yeah, me, too."

"Wanna talk about it?"

She smiled. Good old Vinnie. "When have you known me not to talk, Vinnie?"

"Well," he began as he changed lanes and headed onto the freeway, "there was that time you had your wisdom teeth pulled and they put you under...."

Liz laughed in pure delight.

By the time they returned from the concert later that evening, she had told Vinnie all about Griff and Casie. Vinnie had counseled her to go slowly in this, but then, Vinnie always told her that she was too eager to help out.

"That's your whole problem, you know." He slouched against the open doorjamb. "You think that you can save everyone and make them happy."

"I seem to recall saving a skinny little boy who turned out pretty well," she reminded him.

Vinnie drew himself up and squared his thin shoulders. "Not everyone turns out as sterling as I did."

"That's what I love most about you, Vinnie, your deep humility. Go home and write your reviews," she urged, her hands on his chest as she pretended to push him toward his car. "Good night, Vinnie."

"Uh-huh."

He turned and she knew he didn't even hear her. He was already composing the review that would run in the paper next Tuesday. She let out a contented sigh and closed the door. It had been a very full day and she was more than willing to put it and herself to bed.

With the light in the living room off, the signal on her answering machine blinked at her urgently from its place on the bookcase, like the bloodshot eye of a drunken sailor trying to flirt. Liz slipped out of her shoes and picked them up. It was nearly one o'clock and she wasn't in the mood to call anyone back. She passed the machine and walked into her bedroom, intending to leave the messages until morning.

Curiosity got the better of her.

Liz crossed back to the machine. Pressing the right combination of buttons, she waited to hear her first message. Suddenly, Griff's voice filled the air. It was stiff and uncomfortable and there was another note in it she couldn't quite put a name to.

"This is Griff. Give me a call when you can. I need to talk to you."

Need, now there was an unusual word for him to use, she thought. She was about to discontinue the other two messages and play them back later, but before she could flip the switch, Griff's voice came at her again. This time, he sounded more impatient.

"This is Griff. Where are you? There's something wrong with Casie. Call me."

Concern. That was the note she had detected in the first message. The angry concern in his voice was something new. While it gratified her that she hadn't been wrong about the man's feelings toward Casie, she didn't have time to dwell on it. He needed her and she'd better call back—

The third message clicked in. This time, he was fairly shouting at her. "Damn it, where the hell are you? It's twelve-thirty. If you don't call by one, I'm taking Casie to the emergency room."

God, this *was* serious.

She looked at her watch. Ten to one. Instead of wasting time and calling, she decided to drive straight over. He might be on his way out and not bother to answer the phone. It would only take her five minutes to get to his house. She hurried out, threw her purse and shoes into the car and got in behind the steering wheel.

She barreled into his driveway in three minutes instead of five.

Coming to a screeching halt next to his car, she jumped out of hers just as he was about to get into his. Casie was already inside the car. Liz could hear her crying even though all the doors were closed.

Anger, fear and frustration warred within Griff. He didn't like any of the emotions. He didn't like emotions at all. But he gave in to anger. She had left him to cope with this, knowing that he couldn't, while she went running around town, doing who-knew-what with whom. And dressed fit to kill.

"Where the hell have you been?" he asked accusingly. "On a date?"

Liz shivered and ran her hands up her bare arms. In her hurry, she had left her wrap at home. "Sort of," she tossed off absently. "Never mind that now, what's wrong with Casie?"

"If I knew that," he retorted, glaring, "I wouldn't be taking her to the hospital."

Rather than waste any more time talking to him, Liz elbowed Griff out of the way, opened the car door and leaned into the back seat where Casie sat strapped in and howling.

"What's the matter, honey?" Liz cooed, feeling Casie's forehead. "She's hot."

"I already know that. She's been crying like this since nine and she won't stop. I've changed her, tried to feed her, even sang to her and she just kept crying."

Despite the urgency of the situation, Liz couldn't help reacting to what he told her. "You sang to her?" She couldn't picture it.

"It worked last night," he snapped, cutting short any sort of comment she was going to make.

Liz saw that Casie was rubbing her mouth. She was trying to shove her fist into it. But Griff said he had already fed her, so it wasn't hunger prompting Casie. More than likely, it could only be one thing.

"Well, I'm afraid it's not going to help in this case, at least, not yet." Liz began to undo the car seat's restraining straps.

"What are you doing?"

"Taking her out." She pulled the baby out of the seat and began walking toward the house.

It took a moment before he realized that she was doing exactly what she said. What was wrong with this woman? "I was going to take her to the hospital." Annoyed, he hurried after her.

"I don't think you need to. I think she's just teething."

"Teething?" he echoed. Was that what this was all about? All this noise over teeth? He eyed Liz suspiciously. "Are you sure?"

She nodded. "She's about the right age for her first one. Open the door."

He did. It struck him that Liz was taking a lot upon herself, but he was at his wits' end and the baby needed help. They would settle the issue of who was in charge here later.

"Turn on the light and I'll show you." Once he switched it on, Liz turned the sobbing baby toward it. "I'm sure I'm right."

She put her finger into the little girl's mouth and lightly felt around. She winced as she was rewarded in her search. Casie was biting down.

"See, right there, on the bottom." As gently as she could, Liz pried the baby's mouth open just wide enough to inspect the tiny dot of white emerging on a field of pink. The area around it was swollen. "It's coming in right here."

Griff stared incredulously. "She's making all that noise over a tooth?"

"It hurts like hell, Foster," Liz informed him. She looked around. She remembered seeing a modestly stocked bar around somewhere this afternoon. "Got any whiskey around?"

He stared at her. "Isn't this an odd time to ask for a drink?"

"It's not for me, it's for Casie."

He reacted immediately, taking the baby from her. "Are you crazy?" As far as he was concerned, it was a rhetorical question, but he didn't think she'd be this far off.

The protective gesture he displayed might have been lost on him, but it wasn't on Liz. She tried not to smile. Whether or not he admitted it, he cared about

Casie. "I don't suppose you have any Anbesol lying around?"

"Any what?"

"That's what I thought." Gently she took Casie back from him. "Anbesol is a topical anesthetic that numbs the swollen gum. Whiskey does the same thing. It's the best we can do until morning. Then you can go to the drugstore and get some Anbesol and one of those teethings rings filled with liquid." She saw the strange way he was looking at her. "You put that in the freezer. The frozen liquid soothes her gums when she bites down on it. Now move."

He muttered under his breath as he went to the bar in the family room. Reaching under the counter, he took out an almost full bottle of whiskey. He had never thought in his wildest dreams when he purchased the bottle that it would be used to soothe a baby's sore gum.

Holding the bottle aloft, he marched back into the living room. Liz was sitting on the arm of the sofa with Casie in her lap. The baby was drooling all over and generally making a mess of Liz's dress. She seemed oblivious to it, to everything but comforting the baby. A lot of women would have been horrified at having such a fancy dress stained. His estimation of Liz grudgingly rose another notch.

Griff thrust the bottle toward Liz. "Here."

She glanced at it, then up at him. "In a glass, Foster. I need to wet down my finger."

"And I need to wet down more than that." He went back for a shot glass and poured two fingers' worth into it.

Liz dabbed her finger into the amber liquid, then gently massaged Casie's gum with it. Casie made a horrible face, but the crying went down an octave before it finally faded.

Griff took the glass from her, contemplated it, then downed the remainder of the contents. He had a feeling that he was going to need it tonight, for more than one reason.

Chapter Seven

W ould you like me to spend the night?''

Griff almost choked. Staring at her, he lowered the shot glass slowly as he replayed her words in his head. Had he heard her correctly? He was very aware of the fact that there was a silent drama being played out between them on another more sensual, more basic level. He knew that she knew it, too. But he hadn't expected her to come right out and suggest that they sleep together, especially not after she had just come home from a date with another man. A rather expensive date if the dress she was wearing was any indication as to the kind of places her boyfriend took her to.

He set the shot glass down on the coffee table a little too forcefully. There was an ominous crack when it came in contact with the wood. ''What?''

Casie's crying jag had left him a trifle rattled, Liz decided as she rocked the baby. He looked a little ragged around the edges, which had prompted her to make her offer in the first place.

"Would you like me to spend the night?" she repeated, enunciating every word slowly. "I can take care of Casie for you if she starts crying again. You certainly don't appear to be in any shape to look after her."

"Oh."

He felt embarrassed at his mistake. He should have realized that was what she meant. Maybe she hadn't noticed his overreaction. As to her offer, his natural inclination was to turn it down, but then he stopped himself. The woman had a point. He wasn't cut out for all this. She apparently was. That's why he had called her in the first place, he reminded himself. Where had she been half the night, anyway? He felt the stirrings of jealousy take hold again. He shook them off. No business of his where she went and with whom. No business at all.

So why did he feel so angry?

"You're not exactly dressed for it," he pointed out, unable to contain a touch of sarcasm. "She's drooling all over your dress."

Liz glanced at the wet spots that Casie had created. Her heart sank. This was going to be some cleaning bill. Oh well, she tried to rally herself, there was no use lamenting anyway. "It'll come out eventually and I had no idea that taking care of a teething baby had a dress code." She continued rocking and cuddling Casie against her, and the baby began to settle down. Liz raised her eyes to Griff's face. "Now, do you want me to stay or not?"

He wished that she wouldn't look up at him like that. She looked too damn sexy for her own good. Or his. "Suit yourself."

"Foster, the words are, 'yes, thank you,' not 'suit yourself.'"

He looked as if he wanted to spit lead. But he used the words she fed him, however grudgingly. "Yes," he muttered, "thank you."

"See, Casie, even he can be trained," Liz whispered to the baby with a soft laugh.

He heard what she said, just the way she had meant him to, but he ignored her. He looked at her dress and felt a tinge of guilt. It had undoubtedly cost her an arm and a leg. "I'll pay the cleaning bill." He ran his finger over the stain at her shoulder.

She almost reached up to touch his hand, but stopped herself. It would only make him back off. "No need."

"I said I'd pay for the bill. Why do you like to argue over everything?"

Back to their corners again, she thought. "It keeps the adrenaline flowing. Now," she said, rising to her feet, "which is her room?"

"The room she's *staying* in is over here." He led the way to Sally's bedroom.

Liz was aware of the way he had deliberately reshuffled her words. He was still trying to cling to the fact that he was only taking care of Casie temporarily. Didn't give up easily, this one. Well, neither did she. He was going to open up that fortress he called a heart to both of them before she was through.

* * *

Liz sang and hummed and walked the floor for over an hour until, finally, Casie dropped off to sleep. When Liz emerged from Casie's room, it was ten past two and she was way beyond being tired and onto her third wind.

Thinking that Griff had gone to bed, she began to make her way into the kitchen. Maybe she could fix herself a light snack or at least some coffee.

"You always tiptoe around like that?"

She gasped and swung around. Griff sat on the sofa, one long leg stretched out on the cushion. An unopened book was resting on his thigh. He was watching her. The look in his eyes was unguarded, warm and smoldering. She felt a tingle of electricity before she finally crossed to him.

"I thought you'd be fast asleep by now."

He measured his words. "Your singing kept me up."

She sank down on the couch next to him, a little more cautiously than was her style. She wasn't exactly certain why. She was glad, though, that he had stayed up. The strap on her dress slipped from her shoulder and she pulled it up.

"I didn't know I was that loud."

"You weren't."

Her singing had been low and undeniably sexy. A man couldn't sleep with that going on. It made him want too many things.

"Would you like some coffee?"

She was tempted to make a teasing comment about his finally playing the congenial host, but she didn't want to spoil the moment. "I'd love some."

"Wait here."

She leaned back against the deep cushions. "Need some help?" The offer was made unenthusiastically. Suddenly she was bone tired and she wouldn't mind sitting here for the next twenty-four hours or so.

"I can manage."

"So you keep telling me."

She closed her eyes and raised her feet up on the table. They ached. They were also bare. She laughed softly to herself. In her hurry and concern about Casie, she had forgotten her shoes in the car. She hadn't even noticed until now.

Griff returned with the coffee. He handed Liz one of the steaming mugs. She stared down at it, a surprised expression on her face.

"What's the matter, did I get it wrong?" He sat down again, leaving space between them.

"No. You remembered that I took it with milk."

"So?"

She raised it to her lips and took a sip. "I didn't think you'd notice something like that."

Why was she always finding hidden meanings in things? Why couldn't she just leave it alone? And why *did* he notice every single thing about her? "I'm a policeman, I always notice details." The explanation was more for his benefit than for hers.

"Oh."

He didn't quite like the way her eyes danced behind the mug as she uttered the single word. Why shouldn't he remember how she took her coffee? Just a detail. Like the way her mouth felt against his. Details. Simple, ordinary details.

No, not so simple. Not so ordinary.

Slowly, undeniably, desire poured through his veins, like a relentless demon demanding its due. He ached from it. He ached for her. And there was nothing he could do to stop it.

Except go on the offensive. "Did you leave your shoes at your boyfriend's house?"

She looked at her feet. "No, they're in my car. I had them in my hand when I played back your messages on my answering machine. I guess I forgot to put them on." She wiggled her toes. "You might be good at details, Foster, but you're lousy at conclusions."

He didn't know whether to be relieved that he had been wrong, or wary because it mattered to him that he was. He shrugged nonchalantly. "Well, you're obviously dressed for a date—"

"A concert," she corrected.

"There's a difference?"

She grinned broadly. "There is when you go with Vinnie."

"Vinnie?" he repeated.

She nodded and took another sip before answering. "The man you interrogated me about yesterday."

Mischief lifted the corners of her mouth. He wanted to kiss her into submission. But who would be ultimately submitting to whom was not a foregone conclusion.

Seeing that he was drawing a blank, she gave him another clue. "The photograph on the piano."

"Then he's not your boyfriend." She hadn't made that clear to him yesterday.

"Vinnie and I go back. Way back."

A lover? "How far back?"

She paused deliberately. Don't deny it, Griff Foster, you *are* a little jealous. You do have feelings under that coat of heavy iron mail about your heart. "Really far. To a sandbox."

"What?"

She was talking in riddles again. He liked things cut-and-dried. He doubted she knew the meaning of the words. His coffee was growing cold as he studied the woman on his sofa. *His* sofa, *his* turf. So why did he feel so confused, so awkward?

"We were both eleven. He was being beaten up by a bully and I hit the bully over the head with my social studies book. Made a pretty good-sized dent." She swirled the last of her coffee around in the mug as she talked. "Vinnie pledged his undying loyalty. He's a music critic now and gets free tickets to a lot of programs. I go with him on occasion. We share a love of music." She leaned over and placed her mug on the coffee table. "Have I satisfied your curiosity?"

From this angle, he had a very good view of her breasts. He nearly snapped off the handle on his mug. "I wasn't being curious. Just making conversation."

"Ah."

The single word said it all. He knew she saw right through him and that irritated him almost as much as the fact that he *was* curious about her.

He deliberately changed the subject. "You sure that the only thing wrong with Casie is that she's cutting a tooth?"

He had a lot of good defensive moves, she thought in admiration. "Yup."

"Day care make you such an expert?"

He was trying to be cynical again. Well, it wouldn't work this time. She was beginning to understand him a little better.

"No, four younger brothers and sisters and a cousin who lived with us. I had to take care of them while my parents worked."

Despite himself, he wanted to know more. Maybe, he thought, he wanted some common ground between them. But why, when he was trying to block her out of his life? She had him working at cross-purposes. "You were a latchkey kid?"

"No, not really. I always thought of latchkey kids as being alone and lonely. I wasn't alone and I certainly didn't have the time to be lonely." Lazily, she rubbed one foot against the instep of another. "Besides, my parents were right up-front."

"Up-front?" He tried not to pay attention to what she was doing. She seemed oblivious to the fact that the slitted skirt slipped back further, exposing her legs all the way up to her thighs. He felt himself growing warmer. What would those long legs feel like wrapped around him?

She wondered why he suddenly took such a deep breath. He looked as if he was trying to rouse himself. Was she boring him?

"They ran a mom-and-pop grocery store. A big chain bought them out about five years ago and they retired to San Diego. We have family gatherings there every occasion we can think of. Would you like to come for Christmas?'' She leaned toward him, bridging the space he had so carefully put between them.

She was driving his hormones crazy. Hormones, hell, she was driving *him* crazy. He could smell the light fragrance that she wore. Jasmine. Clean, promising eternal spring after a too-long winter. He longed to bury his face in it.

"I thought you said they were *family* gatherings.''

She smiled at him patiently. "We're allowed to bring in strays. That's what makes Christmas *Christmas*, Griff. Sharing.''

For a moment, just for a moment, he was tempted to find out what it would be like to spend the holidays with a loving family, a family who really cared. But what would be the point? He wasn't part of them. He'd only be on the outside looking in again.

Christmas had no meaning for him. If anything, it had meant a time of intensified hurt and loneliness when he was younger, nothing more. "No, thanks.''

We'll see, she thought, not willing to give up just yet. "Up to you.'' She looked away, wondering what had happened to him to make him like this and what it would take for her to find out.

He paused. "I'm sorry I snapped at you before— when you came in.''

She turned to look at him again. "That's okay. You were worried.''

He shifted, uncomfortable with her assessment. "It's just that she's so small and—''

Liz leaned forward again and put her hand over his. "You don't have to explain, Griff. It's natural to worry about babies. It comes with the territory.''

He pulled his hand back. What he really wanted to do was take hold of her and kiss her until he no longer ached from the desire. But he couldn't let himself do that.

"I didn't stake out the territory."

"No, it seems to have staked you out in this case, but it's still your territory."

He shouldn't have called her. "Not for long."

"So you say."

He should have his head examined for ever thinking she could help—and for thinking what he was thinking right now. It was asking for trouble.

"Do you know you have this damn smug look on your face?"

Her mouth was inches from his. "What are you going to do about it?"

Her breath feathered along his lips. There was just so long he could resist, just so much a man could stand before he broke. "Wipe it off." Griff took hold of her shoulders and pulled her toward him.

"I thought you'd never ask."

It was worse than before. And better. Inconceivably, infinitely better. She had an impact on him that left him shaken and wanting at the same time. He knew he should back away now while there was still time.

He couldn't have stopped himself even if his life depended on it. And maybe it did.

Part witch. She was part witch. There was no other explanation for it, no other explanation for why she was preying on his mind like this, why his self-control, always so strong, seemed to break down each time he

was alone with her. He could blame it on a million
things, but none of it would stick and he knew it. The
thing that did stick was the fact that he couldn't let her
get to him. He couldn't open up. There was nothing
inside to give her.

So where were all those sensations she was stirring
coming from?

His mind told him to end it right now, to move
along, but his body begged him stay. His body and
something else, far away and nebulous. But insistent.

He stayed.

If she had been tired a moment ago, she wasn't any
longer. Every inch of her was awake to what was going
on, to the width and depth of the kiss that claimed
both their souls. Although he tried to keep a distance
between himself and the immediate world with words,
the man who was kissing her now, whose hands
molded her body to his, was vulnerable and sensitive
and everything that Griff tried to tell her he wasn't.

He rose to his feet, pulling her up with him. She felt
his desire, hard and hot. It excited her beyond all
normal bounds. She pressed against him, reveling in
the world he was creating for them.

It was need and power, possession and submission,
all rolled up into one. If she was being reckless, she'd
pay the price later. Now there was nothing but this
feeling he generated within her. So sweet, so painful.
She didn't want to lose it, no matter what it cost her.
She didn't want to lose him.

His head reeled from all that he took from her. And
still there was more, so much more. He couldn't get
enough. He needed it to breathe, to feel alive. It was

as if his soul was emerging out of some deep, dark cave into the bright sunlight.

Was he crazy? Had he lost his mind? He was babbling nonsense to himself and yet that was the way he felt, as though he were bathed in sunlight after an eternity of darkness. He sounded like a kid. Like some damned adolescent trembling on the brink of his first love.

Love.

He moved back from her so abruptly she nearly pitched forward.

Liz struggled to catch her breath. "Was—was it something I said?" she asked in a hoarse whisper, her eyes wide.

It took a minute to refocus, a long minute to fight the urge to sweep her back into his arms, to get her out of that maddening dress with its beads that pressed against his flesh, and into his bed.

"We shouldn't be doing this."

She refused to show her disappointment, but that didn't mean she didn't need to know what made him turn from her so suddenly. She had felt his passion. It was no less than her own. "Why?"

Because I can't love you, he answered silently to himself. I can't love anything. It's all dead inside.

But he couldn't tell her that.

"Do you always have to ask questions?" he retorted.

"It helps to clear things up. Although in your case, I'm not so sure." She fought to keep her emotions from spilling out. Hurt feelings weren't going to help.

Almost afraid to, Liz reached out and put her hand on his shoulder. "Griff, I'd like to understand."

He shrugged off her hand. "Understand what?"

Because he wouldn't turn to face her, she walked around until she faced him. "What it is you're afraid of. It can't be me."

The hell it can't. "I'm not afraid of anything. You don't know what you're talking about."

Look at me, Griff. Look at *me*. "Then tell me."

"It's late—"

"It was late five minutes ago. That doesn't change the subject."

"You're making something out of nothing."

He struggled to sound as though what had just happened between them hadn't shaken him to the core of his existence, hadn't made him face his devils and come up wanting.

"You're attractive. You're falling out of your dress," he told her, trying to pull himself back into control. "And maybe I got a little carried away."

For a moment, she hated him for the wall he was putting between them. Glaring at him, Liz pulled up the sinking décolletage.

"Besides, men kiss women all the time."

He began to walk toward his bedroom. She was obviously not invited.

Quickly, Liz stepped around in front of him and put her hand on his chest to keep him in his place. There was now fire in her eyes. "Yes, they do. But you're forgetting something."

No, not a damn thing could be forgotten, not the way your body feels, or your mouth, or the honey in your hair. Or the fact that it will all turn to ashes if I reach for it. "What?"

"I was there for that kiss, Foster. That wasn't 'nothing.' You didn't exactly phone it in."

Don't, Liz. Let it go. For both our sakes. "It was purely physical."

"Not exclusively." As she was tossing her head, the remaining pins in her hair came loose and the sea of blond silk finally tumbled down to her shoulders. He almost reached out to touch it, to run it through his fingers. He clenched his fists at his sides. "What makes you such an expert?"

She looked him squarely in the eye, daring him to deny it. "Intuition."

He did. "Well, your intuition is wrong."

Liz shook her head. "I don't think so. Tell me you didn't feel anything just then."

It was easy to say the words as long as he didn't look at her warm and tempting mouth. "I didn't feel anything."

"I don't believe you."

"That's your problem." He looked at her and knew he had lost. "And mine." She was more than his match. He seized her into his arms. "Damn you, anyway...."

Laughter highlighted her eyes. "That's the nicest thing anyone's ever said to me."

Because it was the only way to stop her mouth, he kissed her. Kissed her long and hard with all the loneliness and longing that he had suddenly become aware of. There were barriers within him, barriers that begged to be freed. He couldn't free them, couldn't let them loose. But for a moment, for one brief, shining moment, he could give in to temptation.

He wanted to lose himself in her. To pretend that the past hadn't happened, to pretend that his life had begun the moment she had swept into it, sliding past that stop sign in that dusty, absurd little car of hers.

But he couldn't. Not for long. The past had too good a hold on him, had been forged out of too strong a steel to give up its grip. He was a product of it.

He was who he was and he knew that there were no happy endings, not in this life. Not for him. If you gave your heart, it was returned, more than slightly damaged and totally unwanted. He had learned that lesson over and over again until he had sworn to himself that no one and nothing would ever hurt him again.

Especially not a woman with lips that tasted of all the sweet things he had ever longed for when he was still young enough to dream.

She sensed the withdrawal, could *feel* him thinking.

Don't think, damn you, feel. For once in your life, *feel*, she wanted to cry. But she knew she couldn't hurry him, or them. That was a step that was going to have to evolve. Just like trust.

He took her face between his hands and looked down into her eyes. He saw his reflection mirrored there, small and lost. Yes, he could get lost there—at a price. "I think it's time for bed."

She smiled, letting him know that she understood—even if she didn't entirely. "I'll be in Casie's room if you need me."

He watched her go.

I *do* need you, Liz. But it would be the worst thing in the world for me to give in to that.

Quietly, he switched off the light and went to bed alone.

Chapter Eight

Coffee?

Was that coffee that he smelled?

No, he had to be still dreaming. He was in his own bed. Coffee didn't just make itself.

As the early-morning haze of sleep began to lift from his brain, the aroma of coffee continued to seep into his room. Subconsciously, his mind related the presence of coffee to there being something different, something out of the norm happening.

And then he remembered.

She was still here.

It *was* coffee.

Griff bolted upright, knocking the blanket off his bare shoulders.

There was a knock on his door just as last night came back to him. Liz. A thousand jumbled thoughts and feelings assaulted him at once. It was too early to deal with any of them. Or her. Even fresh and alert, he had difficulty dealing with her.

"Foster, are you decent—clotheswise I mean?" It was basically a simple, honest question. Yet just the sound of her low, whiskey-smoldering voice wafting through the door unsettled him. "I already have the answer to any other meaning."

Six-thirty in the morning and she was already making wisecracks. It figured.

"Yeah." He ran his hand through his hair, wishing he had time to pull himself together mentally before facing her, then decided that there probably wasn't that much time available in the world. "Listen, why don't you come back in a few—?"

She didn't wait for him to finish his sentence. The word *come* was all she needed. She opened the door and took a step in, then stopped. Griff was sitting up in bed, the blanket gathered down around his waist. He was naked from the waist up, possibly from the waist down, she thought as a warm, electric sensation danced through her. With his hair in his eyes and sleep etching his face, he still exuded sensuality from every pore. Liz stayed where she was, telling her pulse to settle down.

He hadn't thought she'd come barging in, but then, he knew he should have. That she remained in the doorway seemed almost out of character, but he was grateful for it. She wasn't alone, either. On her hip, resting comfortably as if she had been created there, was Casie. The baby was obviously in better spirits than she had been last night. But it wasn't Casie who held his attention. It was Liz. She was wearing a bathrobe.

Liz saw him staring at her. She looked down, following his line of vision. "Oh, this," she answered his silent inquiry, hoping that she didn't sound too flustered. "I found it hanging in the bathroom. I hope you don't mind, but I couldn't see fixing breakfast in a beaded dress."

He conjured up a vision of her doing just that. It had its pluses. But so did seeing her in his bathrobe. It fit her like a navy-blue pup tent and gave every indication that it was going to slip off her shoulders if she made any sudden movements. He wondered what she was wearing underneath it. He felt desire surge through his loins and forced his mind elsewhere. That worked for about half a minute.

Casie tugged at the sash that was lightly tied at Liz's waist. Liz grabbed it before it had a chance to unceremoniously come apart.

"You do eat breakfast, don't you? Or do you just get up and begin growling on an empty stomach?"

Casie was tenacious, Griff noticed. He wondered if Liz was aware that the baby was now making an effort to disentangle the other side of the sash. Maybe he should tell her. Later. "I eat breakfast."

What was he looking at? Was something showing? She doubted it. She felt positively enshrouded in his bathrobe. The tops of her feet barely showed. "Is there anything in particular you want?"

Yeah. "Whatever's handy."

She saw a smile begin to grow on his lips. Now what was that about? "I've seen the cereal box. The cereal's

stale," she pronounced. "I threw the last of it out."
She saw his eyebrows go up. Quickly, she tried to
forestall his annoyance. "French toast strike your
fancy?"

"French toast?" he echoed absently, intent on
watching Casie tug on the sash.

Liz suddenly became aware of what was going on.
Shifting the slipping Casie higher on her hip, she almost lost her dignity completely. Casie gurgled as she
yanked the sash off. Liz grabbed for the two sides of
the robe, which had parted company now that the sash
lay on the floor at her bare feet.

She saw desire flash in Griff's eyes.

She bent down awkwardly, still holding Casie.
Snatching up the sash, she managed to work it back
around her waist. "Now keep those busy little hands
off," she reprimanded Casie affectionately. Then she
turned to look at Griff who was watching her with an
amused expression. "As for you, you could have
averted your eyes, officer Foster." She tried to sup-
press the warm, pleased feeling she had, even as it
warred with her embarrassment.

"Yeah, I could have." He gave no indication that
he would have done anything of the kind.

Elaborately, she took hold of the two ends of the
sash and twisted them around tightly in her hand so
that Casie could no longer play with them. "So, you're
human after all."

Only too human as far as you seem to be concerned, he thought with a touch of annoyance as well
as interest. "Human enough to want that French toast
you just offered."

The way his eyes appraised her, she knew he didn't have French toast on his mind.

Neither did she, but this wasn't the time or the place to explore what was silently going on between them. Maybe later, she thought with a touch of sadness, wishing she were a little more reckless or that Casie had slept just a little bit longer.

"Right. French toast coming up." She marched off, her hips unintentionally swaying provocatively beneath the terry-cloth robe.

Griff watched the easy rhythm of the sway. Damn, he wanted her. Though it was wrong and would never work, he wanted her in the worst way. But he knew he couldn't handle the added complications. He was having enough trouble just dealing with having Casie pop up unexpectedly in his life. He'd seen what had happened to policemen with emotional problems at home. They lost their edge. He couldn't allow that to happen—not for any reason—not even in a town with as little crime as Bedford.

"Don't hurry, I have to take a shower first." A cold one, he added mentally.

He heard Liz laugh softly to herself and wondered if she could read his thoughts. It certainly wouldn't have been hard at the moment.

When he had finished with his shower and had gotten dressed, Griff felt as if he was once more in control of himself.

Walking into the kitchen, he realized that he was living in a fool's paradise. Or maybe that was where he wanted to live. To fool himself for a little while and pretend that everything wasn't the way it was.

She was standing there, barefoot up to the neck, he mused longingly, with his bathrobe covering her long, tan legs and sleek athletic body. The fact that he had worn that bathrobe against his own body just yesterday morning heightened the degree of intimacy between them to a point he didn't think possible.

Her hair was piled up high on her head in a haphazard ponytail, with tendrils tumbling down every which way. She looked absolutely delectable. A witch in total control of the situation and an imp partially at his mercy at the same time. He didn't know which he wanted more, he only knew that he wanted her.

"I missed my bathrobe," he murmured as he crossed the room to her. Off to the left, Casie sat making a mess in her new high chair. It was a domestic scene straight out of a Norman Rockwell portrait, he thought.

And yet there was this current of electricity running through it so strongly that he felt he could touch it if he tried.

He wanted to touch her. She was making him crazy.

For a moment, from the tone of his voice, she thought that he was going to demand that she return his robe right then and there. "You should have more than one," she answered, trying to ignore the way her heart was pounding at his nearness. He was right behind her and she could have sworn that she felt the heat of his body.

"There's never been a need to before last night."

She turned around, her body brushing against his, feeding the flame between them. "Don't you, um—" she ran her tongue against her dry lips "—entertain?"

"Is that what they call it, now?" With very little encouragement, he could easily separate her from the bathrobe. He was strongly debating the possibility. "You're probing again."

"Yes," she said softly, "I am." She searched his eyes for an answer.

"No," he told her needlessly. She already knew his answer, yet hearing it from him made her glad.

"I'm surprised."

"I didn't think you could be surprised."

"Yes," she said, rising on her toes, her breath touching his lips. "Every once in a while. Surprise me."

"Okay."

He turned and began to walk away.

She stared, stunned, wanting to throw the frying pan at him. How could he lead her on this way, knowing, unless he was totally blind, how she felt about him? How vulnerable she was right now?

Griff swung around on his heel and took her into his arms so fast her breath whooshed out of her.

"Surprise," he murmured against her mouth just before he kissed her.

Drunk. There was no other way to describe it. He made her feel drunk and dizzy and created a thousand different contradictory sensations within her. It was too wonderful to put into words. And he wanted her, she knew it. It was only when he kissed her that she felt she was getting to the true man, the man beneath the scowl and solemn words. The man who spoke to her soul.

Griff slipped his hands beneath the robe. She wasn't wearing anything under it, just as he had fantasized. The feel of her soft skin made him ache so badly that he didn't think he could withstand the temptation to make love to her right here, right now.

He only allowed his hands to span her waist. But his long fingers dipped low on her back, skimming the sensitive area of her buttocks. Without thinking, only feeling, he pressed her against him. He heard her gasp again, then moan his name against his mouth just as her passion rose to entwine with his.

It was all going too fast for him. He needed time, time to sort things out, time to think. And he couldn't think, not with her in his arms.

This was madness and any second he was going to be washed away with it.

Somehow, she had snuck past all his safeguards and struck at the very core of his being. He had vowed never to want again, never to love again. Never to offer his heart again. He had suffered his affections being rejected time and again as he and Sally were passed around from one family to another like so much loose change. He had hardened his heart, sworn that he needed no one. And he hadn't.

Not until now.

He didn't like having feelings. He didn't trust them. Feelings led you astray. Feelings complicated things, left you vulnerable, got in the way of functioning.

Feelings involved you in a way that he didn't want to be involved.

But he didn't seem to have any choice.

His mouth drained her of everything she had to give and yet there was more, always more. She had no idea where it was coming from. She just knew that she wanted to give it all to him. Maybe it had been stored up, just waiting to be set free. Just waiting for someone like him. Someone strong, someone dependable.

Just waiting for him.

She entangled her fingers in his hair, pulling him closer to her, uttering a small, animal-like cry when he began to kiss her cheek, her ear, then the sensitive part of her throat. In another moment, she knew she was going to slip past the point of no return.

She didn't care. She wanted him, wanted to be wanted by him. Nothing else mattered.

She yelped, pushing against Griff. This time driven by pain rather than passion.

"What the—?"

She turned and looked back at the stove. The oil had heated and was now angrily dancing high off the pan. She had forgotten to turn the flame down, forgotten everything but the man who so effectively blotted out the rest of the world for her.

Seeing the potential danger, Griff quickly elbowed her aside, pulling the pan off the flame and onto a cold burner. He threw a cover over the pan. The oil sizzled beneath it, pinging a symphony of anger. "We almost burned the house down."

She leaned against the counter, as much for support as anything. She pulled together her disarrayed robe. "Among other things."

He forced back his hunger. He had no business losing control like that. "If this is an example of how you cook, maybe I'll just have some juice."

The moment was gone, but the memory was going to live on a long time. They were both on the threshold of something, something wondrous and very frightening at the same time, and she had a feeling that he knew it, too.

"Coward," she scoffed softly.

He held up his hands and there was a smile on his lips, but his eyes told her that he understood what she was talking about. And it wasn't about her culinary skills.

"Guilty as charged." He passed Casie and picked up the spoon she had thrown on the floor.

Casie reached for it as he stood up, and wrapped her fist around it. Metal met high chair and she used the spoon to produce her own brand of music.

He wanted it, wanted all of this: Casie, her, commitment. She could sense it. Why did he fight it so hard? "Courage is proceeding on even when you're afraid of what lies ahead."

He met Liz's eyes only briefly. "Sounds good." With studied nonchalance, Griff opened the refrigerator and took out a container of orange juice. "I'll try to remember that."

He turned and saw that she was scrutinizing him intently. There was no hiding his thoughts from her, he realized in annoyance as he raised the glass to his lips.

"See that you do," Liz said and then began to make a fresh serving of French toast.

After breakfast Liz sent Griff off to the drugstore with a list of things intended to see Casie through another siege of tooth-cutting pain. On the whole, the little girl seemed to settle down.

But Griff couldn't. He could handle Casie keeping him awake, he thought to himself as he drove off, a lot better than he could handle having Liz walking about wearing his bathrobe, unconsciously tempting him until he thought he would lose all reason.

When he returned from the drugstore Liz was wearing her rose dress again. He was relieved.

And just the least bit regretful.

As soon as he had given her the bag from the drugstore, Liz sat him down and began to go over what to check for if Casie were to act up again. He sat there, dutifully trying to absorb all the details she was throwing at him. He was also trying very hard *not* to notice the way the morning sunlight streaming in through the kitchen window seemed to get itself caught in her hair.

"What are you staring at?" she finally asked.

He attempted to gloss over it by sounding matter-of-fact. "Do you know that there are red streaks in your hair when the sun hits it?"

"Those are called highlights."

And what do you call the streaks running through me every time I'm near you? he asked silently. He had the answer for that himself: insanity.

Liz showed him how to get the better part of a jar of baby food into Casie's mouth, not into her clothes or her hair. She showed him how to change Casie without using half the towels in his linen closet to clean up the mess that seemed to be a by-product of this process when he tackled it. She showed him a great many things, predominantly what it was that he had been missing all his life.

And what it was that he knew he could never have.

It was useless to even contemplate a commitment between them. He could never overcome the enclosure that held his emotions hostage. He might have momentary breakthroughs, but he wasn't the kind who could show feelings. And Liz, he could tell, was the type who needed to feel surrounded by love. He couldn't give that to her. There was no point in his even dwelling on it.

"Well, thanks a lot," he mumbled awkwardly as Liz began to take her leave.

"Sounds like you're thanking the plumber for coming over to fix a leak," she noted philosophically, "but it's a start."

And so is the way you kissed me in the kitchen, Liz added silently. The sparks in the frying pan weren't the only ones that flew. "See you two tomorrow."

"Yeah."

She wanted him to say something further, or do something, but he merely stood there, waiting for her to leave. So she did.

Rome wasn't built in a day, she told herself, and she *had* made progress. If that errant spark of oil hadn't smacked her in the posterior just when it had, she had a feeling that Officer Griffin Foster would have taken quite a quantum jump forward in personal relations this morning. Those emotions he held back so fiercely had nearly escaped then. She knew that with him it wouldn't be just a matter of two bodies joining. If it were, he had had ample opportunity to make some sort of a move before now. And if that had been the case, he wouldn't have attracted her the way he did. No, with Griff the act of lovemaking was tied in with feelings, with caring. She would have staked her life on it.

Liz gripped the handle on her car door and pulled. Nothing happened. She tried again, then realized that the car was locked. And her keys were in her purse. She remembered that as she looked down at her evening bag. It was innocently nestled on the front seat next to her shoes. Behind the locked door.

Liz sighed and leaned her head against the door for a moment. Done in once again by the fact that she was always hurrying. This time, at least, there had been a legitimate reason for haste.

That didn't help her now.

Griff, she thought suddenly. Griff was a policeman, right? He could easily get the door open for her. She turned around and marched back up the walk.

Griff had just picked Casie up out of her playpen. She was beginning to moan again. "Know she's gone, right?" he asked the child. "Well, this time we're going to muddle through by ourselves. I know what to do now." He heard the knock. "Now what?"

He crossed to the door and opened it, not knowing what to expect. No one paid social calls on him and it was Sunday, so there would be no neighborhood children trying to sell him candy he didn't want or wrapping paper he didn't need.

Liz was standing on the doorstep. "Did you hear her moaning?" he asked incredulously.

"No, I locked myself out of my car. Are you in pain again, Casie?" she asked.

He handed the baby to her. "Nothing I can't handle. Wait right here."

"I'm not going anywhere," she called after him.

It took him five minutes and a bent coat hanger to get the door open for her. She grinned as she passed Casie back to him. The baby was biting down on the ice-blue teething ring Liz had fetched from the freezer. "It's nice to have connections in the right places."

He looked at the teething ring. "I was just thinking the same thing."

Then, to his surprise, he bent and kissed her goodbye lightly on the lips. Somehow, with Casie in his arms, it seemed the thing to do.

Liz drove off, knowing that it had finally happened and it was time she called it by its rightful name. She rolled down her windows and called out, "Hey, world! Elizabeth Ann MacDougall has fallen in love."

There was no one in the street to hear her, but it didn't diminish the magnitude of the statement, or the way she felt.

* * *

"Hey, hey, there he is!" C.W. called out as Griff came into the locker room early Monday morning. "Boy, you sure had us fooled." C.W. stretched a little as he laughed and clapped Griff on the back.

To Griff's dismay, several other officers gathered around them.

His glance barely acknowledged C.W. "Would you like to explain that?" Griff's voice was low, and he knew that normally the others quietly backed off when he spoke in that tone.

Today, it didn't work. Or maybe the tone he was using didn't sound menacing enough or have as much conviction behind it as it usually did.

C.W. just went on talking to the other men as if nothing had been said. "He's got himself an instant family there, baby and all."

"The baby belongs to my sister." Griff uttered the statement between clenched teeth.

These people didn't belong in his private life. No one did, he tried to tell himself firmly. An image of Liz shimmered in his mind's eye. Liz, wearing his bathrobe and holding Casie.

"Didn't know you had a sister, Griff," a young officer said.

Griff turned slightly to look at the shorter man. "The subject never came up." The look Griff gave him should have silenced them all.

It didn't.

"A lot of things haven't come up." C.W. winked. "Like, where've you been hiding that cute little number we saw you with. Liz, isn't it?"

Griff opened his locker, trying to ignore the men around him. "I wasn't hiding her. She's taking care of Casie for me during the day."

Ernie jockeyed himself into position in front of Griff. "What she doing for you at night, Griff?" A wide grin split his face.

"Aren't you due out on patrol, Ernie?"

But his abrupt tone had no effect on the two policemen, or any of the others who were listening.

"Let me know if you need any pointers, Griff," Ernie called over his shoulder as he went out, chuckling.

Griff swore under his breath, but not nearly as vehemently as he thought the situation warranted. Maybe she was getting to him after all.

And maybe there was no maybe about it.

Something would have to be done about that, he promised himself. Later.

Chapter Nine

It had crept up on him. Somehow, when he hadn't been paying attention, love with its steel-binding nylon tentacles had networked all through his soul, hopelessly enmeshing him and taking him prisoner.

He thought he had shored up his defenses rather well and that he was impervious to any assault. He had thought wrong. The walls had been breached with surprising ease. A child had managed it.

Griff looked down at his niece as she slept in her crib. She had been part of his life for a month now and in that time she had grown. In size. He had grown as well, grown emotionally. Liz had been right. He *did* care about the little girl. It would have taken a very hard heart not to, a heart like the ones he encountered when he was growing up. Ones with no love in them, at least not for him. The families he had been forced to stay with had been concerned with him only because he meant a monthly stipend from the government and another pair of working hands at home. He had meant nothing more to any of them. And he had gotten nothing more from them even when he had been willing to give. So willing at first. And then he had dammed his love up.

Until now.

A small smile spread across his face as he moved the covers over Casie's shoulders. She never seemed to stay covered no matter how large a blanket he used and how many times he placed it on her during the night.

Casie lay on her stomach, curled up with the stuffed animal he had just happened to pick up yesterday on his way to Liz's house. Buying the toy had been totally out of character for him. He was doing a lot of things that were totally out of character for him of late.

He wasn't sure yet if he was comfortable with the change, he thought as he slipped out softly.

Liz was in the kitchen, making dinner. He wasn't sure just how that had come about, either. She had just appeared on his doorstep, groceries in hand. These days it seemed that she was always somewhere close by, in sight or if not, in mind. She haunted the caverns of his mind a lot and there too the odds were beginning to turn against him. He suspected that he didn't have a prayer against her, against the emotions she always seemed to churn up within him.

He stood in the doorway, silently watching her as she moved easily about his kitchen preparing dinner for the two of them. They saw each other every day.

During the week it was because he had to drop off Casie in the morning and then pick her up again at night. Weekends he didn't have that excuse to hide behind. Once he'd set his mind to it, he'd learned rather quickly how to take care of Casie. He knew he didn't need to call Liz for help. And yet time and again, he found himself doing just that, using some triviality as an excuse. As hard as he tried to disguise his reason, he knew he was just rationalizing. He *wanted* to see her, wanted to be with her.

His need for Liz made him ill at ease. It wasn't like him. He had spent so much effort, so much time perpetuating his shell and here she was penetrating it. With his help. If he didn't need, he didn't get hurt. If he didn't have expectations, he couldn't be disappointed.

Why couldn't he remember that around her?

Liz didn't seem to need excuses. She just popped up, like tonight. She always seemed content and at ease with her actions.

But he wasn't that uninhibited, that unreserved. Twenty years of keeping his feelings in rigid check was a lot to conquer and there were times he doubted that he could do it, or that he had anything of value to offer someone as special as Liz.

Or that he could stand it if it all blew up on him, the way he firmly believed in his heart that it was destined to.

He knew he should leave before the roof caved in, for both their sakes, and yet, he just couldn't seem to make himself do it.

"You know that old adage about a watched pot never boiling?" Liz didn't bother to look up in his direction. Yet she knew the exact moment he had appeared in the doorway. She could sense his presence. It seemed to fill up the space around her.

He wondered how she knew he was there. He remembered hearing once that there were souls who were fated for each other, chosen at the beginning of time. Kindred spirits. Was that the answer?

No, he told himself, that was just a silly, romanticized theory. Yet she still knew.

Griff remained leaning against the doorjamb. "What about the old adage?"

"It goes for a watched cook."

"You were planning on boiling?" he asked, amused.

She turned in his direction and batted her lashes at him in an exaggerated manner. "That depends on what you had in mind after dinner." With her free hand, she reached for the colander to drain the spaghetti.

It would be so easy, so very easy to slip into a pattern, to let himself pretend that this could go on forever, just the three of them. A home. A family. Wasn't that what he had once yearned for?

Yes, and what he had been continually shown that he couldn't have. The realization, finally hammered home, had drained him, had made him empty. He didn't have what she needed, what she deserved. It was too late for him.

The spaghetti could wait. This was more important.

"You're frowning again."

"Sorry." He straightened and crossed to the table she had set. Ever efficient. A whirlwind on legs.

"Don't be sorry." Quickly, because it was getting sticky, she rinsed the spaghetti and set it aside. "Talk. What are you frowning about?" Deftly, she switched off the sauce she had prepared. Picking up a knife, she began to slice small bits of cheese to use as garnish.

Griff sat down on a chair and leaned back. "Nothing."

She sighed. "'Nothing' again." She came up to him, waving the paring knife in front of her as an extension of her words. "You know, I've told you my entire life story and I still don't know anything about you other than the fact that you're a policeman, you have a niece and are very protective of a sister you won't talk about."

Griff shrugged, unaffected. *I can't let you into my life any more than I already have, Liz. Even that's too much.* "That's enough to go on."

Her eyes narrowed beneath the wispy bangs. "No, it's not."

Taking her wrist, he tactfully directed the knife she held away from him. "You get a bit too animated for my taste."

She put the knife down on the kitchen table behind her. "You're changing the subject."

Obviously she wasn't going to let him. "And not doing very well at it," he added, growing more somber. "There's nothing to tell."

She saw the way tension outlined his jaw, making it almost rigid. Oh, yes, there was, there was a lot to tell.

She continued to cajole gently, even though she wanted to take him by the shoulders and shake some sense into him. Why wouldn't he share himself with her? Why did he have to keep a part of him locked away? Didn't he know she only wanted to help him?

"There has to be something to tell." She smoothed down the kitchen towel she was using as a makeshift apron. "You didn't just drop out of the sky a month ago. You have to have a past."

"That's just what it is, Liz. Past. Gone. Dead. Leave it there."

His eyes told her to drop the subject, but she couldn't. She returned to the sauce and stirred it in silence for a moment, thinking. "You weren't very happy in the past, were you?"

"No."

"Why?"

"It's no concern of yours."

"So you keep telling me." She swung around in exasperation. The spaghetti pot rattled on the counter as she accidentally hit the protruding handle. She pushed it back farther without even looking at it. "And maybe it isn't. And maybe I should have my head examined for caring enough to *be* concerned." She bit down on her lower lip, biting back a few swear words she would have liked to heap on his head, words that would change nothing. "But I am concerned. I want to know."

He couldn't understand. He kept fighting her at every turn, and still she kept coming. Like Rodan in those ridiculous Japanese movies. Except that she wasn't an ugly, twenty-foot-tall creature. But she still had the power to destroy him.

"Why?"

She wondered how he would look wearing dinner instead of eating it. "Because I care, you big idiot!"

He forced himself to look away from her.

"Don't."

"Easy for you to say," she cried bitterly. "But it doesn't change anything. I still care."

He had to see her face. Maybe he could understand if he looked at her face. "Why?"

She crossed to him and put her hands on either side of the chair he sat on. Her face was inches away from his. "Because I think you need someone to care."

A distant memory stirred within him. Those were almost the exact words the social worker had used when she had told Sally and him that they were going to stay with a foster family. "And you've appointed yourself."

She heard the sarcasm and knew it was his defense mechanism. It's not working Griff, she told him silently. "That's me. A committee of one." She forced herself to smile as she searched his face for some sign that he understood, that he would open up to her if she worked at it hard enough.

He threaded his hands through her hair, framing her face. "You're going to get hurt."

"My decision."

She was making it hard, so very hard to keep away. He wanted to love her, wanted to try, but couldn't. Something wouldn't let him. Fear. "I don't believe in long-term obligations."

"Oh?" Her mouth curved in amusement. She no longer believed that, even if he thought he did.

"Yes, 'oh.'" He kissed her eyes closed one at a time. His actions belied his words.

Her head began to swim. She hurt with needs that only he could soothe. "Then whose baby is that in the next room?"

He knew where she was going with this and he didn't want her to. "My sister's." Griff rose abruptly. She didn't back away an inch. Not in distance, not in cause. She stood with him, toe-to-toe.

Liz smiled smugly and crossed her arms before her. "I rest my case."

"You have no case."

"No?"

"No."

Liz rocked back and forth on her toes. "If you say so."

Her knowing, smug tone got to him. What made her think she had all the answers? "You're just supposed to look after my niece, not me."

"Yes, sir."

She was infuriating, exasperating, and he wanted to make love to her all night long. She was making him feel for the first time in a long time. And the strangest thing of all was that he didn't seem to mind. "I don't need taking care of."

"No, sir."

Her solemn tone broke the tension and he laughed. He put his arms around her. "Why do I get the distinct impression that you're only humoring me and intend to go on doing what you damn well please?"

She turned her face up to his. "Because you're not as dumb as you try to sound, sir."

"Oh, Liz, Liz, what in the world am I going to do with you?"

"Many suggestions come to mind," she said softly. "Trust me, is one." He stiffened ever so slightly, but she felt it nonetheless. Still too raw? she wondered.

Even if I were willing, he thought, I can't. "You're asking a lot."

Liz ran her hands along the front of his shirt. She felt his heart beneath her fingertips. If only she could make it open up to her. "I know, but I'm willing to give a lot."

He took her hands in his to stop her. The touch of her fingers along his skin made it hard for him to concentrate. "I said no strings, Liz."

She pretended to look around. "I don't see any lassos lying around."

"You've already got me tied up in knots." He had no idea what made him admit that. She had some sort of power over him that seemed to supersede his own.

"Tell me more. This is beginning to sound good."

A man could wander into that smile of hers and get himself very lost with no effort at all. He was beginning to believe that had happened to him. "Hog-tied and lassoed. You're turning me every which way but loose."

She shook her head. "It's not me who's doing it. It's you. No one can do anything to you that you won't let them do."

The smile on his face slowly turned bitter as he remembered glints of memories from the past. Horrible memories that were better off buried. "Maybe you're right at that. Then I shouldn't let it happen again." I won't risk wanting love, he added silently.

What had happened to him to make him so bitter? "I think it would only be fair if you told me just what it is that's standing between us. An ex-lover? An ex-wife? What?" The teasing tone had left her voice. "Griff, please, I have to know."

He looked away and she swore he was trying to regain control.

"It's nothing that simple."

If it wasn't a woman, then what was it? Tell me. Griff, please tell me.

When he looked down at her face, he saw the hurt in her eyes, saw the questions there. Without thinking, he hugged her to him. God, he wished he *could* open up. But that part of him was damaged. "Why don't you have a lover?"

"What!" She twisted back and stared at him.

Griff ran his fingers through the tips of her hair. "Why aren't you ugly? Why do you have to prey on my mind so much?"

She smiled warmly, relaxing. "Do I? Do I really?"

"Yes." He traced the curve of her cheek lightly. "Really."

"Go on, this is getting better."

He shook his head. "Just for one of us."

What would it take to make him trust her? To make Griff feel the way she did? "Why are you so afraid of feeling?"

"Because it costs," he answered honestly. "Costs too damn much."

"Everything costs. It costs *not* to feel. The payment is loneliness."

"I can handle that," he said flatly.

"Can you?"

"Yes," he said quietly. "I can handle loneliness and despair. I've gotten used to the despair. I don't mind it enshrouding my days." His eyes touched her face, memorizing it, making love to it. "I don't want to hope, to build again. Don't you understand, Liz? If I let you in, then someday I'll have to suffer the pain of letting you go."

"Oh, Griff," she cried softly, "I already *am* in."

He seized her back into his arms and kissed her with all the passion in his soul. He knew that what she said was true. But rather than admit it, he blotted out his thoughts with the feel of her mouth against his.

In his mind he swore, at her, at himself, at everything in his past that had made him the way he was, trapped him behind a mesh wall that refused to let his emotions out.

Anger, passion, need. What was he feeling? She didn't know. She didn't care. He was reacting to her and that was all that mattered. With so little effort, he took possession of her body and soul. She gave it willingly.

And then he was pulling away again. She almost cried out to stop him. It cost her not to. But she didn't.

He put his hands on her shoulders, as much to steady himself as to keep her back. "Liz, I think you'd be better off if—"

"I served dinner before it burned," she filled in quickly.

There was denial in his eyes. She wasn't going to let him shut her out of his life, not after she had come so far. She wasn't going to let him tell her to go away. She had pushed too hard this time. So be it. She could wait. There'd be other openings, and perhaps it would be easier for him to tell her some other time.

It wasn't easy, but she pretended as if nothing had happened just now, as if her soul hadn't been on fire with need. Busying herself at the stove, she managed to buy some time to pull her emotions together.

When she turned around, her expression was sunny. "Listen, I've been meaning to ask you." She set down a huge bowl of spaghetti in the center of the small table. "Have you found a doctor for Casie?"

"No. Why? She's not sick." Avoiding her eyes, he helped himself to a serving of pasta.

The man knew nothing. "Babies need a pediatrician for well-baby checkups."

That didn't make any sense to him. "If they're well, why do they—?"

She sat down to join him. "Shots, Foster. They need preventive shots. Did your sister tell you anything about the care Casie's had?" She carefully ladled out some sauce, but her mind was a million miles away from food.

"No." He saw the disapproving look on Liz's face. "Look, I don't want to talk about my sister."

Her temper flared. "I know. There's not a heck of a lot you *do* want to talk about, but I think we should at least discuss Casie." She bit her lip. "Sorry. I didn't mean to blow up like that. I always get emotional when I make pasta."

She broke the tension and he laughed. "Liz, if they could bottle you—"

She leaned her head on an upturned palm as if she were giving him her undying attention. "Yes?"

He pulled back a lock of her hair that threatened to find its way into the sauce. "Then maybe I could take you in small doses. Anyway, you're right. I should get a doctor for her. Will you help me?"

"Sure. Griff, you know what?"

"What?"

"You didn't choke on the word help this time. I think we're beginning to make real progress here despite your pigheadedness."

He pushed her plate toward her. "Eat your pasta."

"Yes, sir."

Liz found a highly recommended pediatrician for Casie the next day and took it upon herself to make an appointment. She informed Griff about it when he came to pick Casie up that evening.

He stared at her. Didn't this woman ever stop steamrolling through his life? "Didn't you even think of asking me?"

She slipped a jacket on Winston. His mother would be coming to pick him up any minute. "Why?" She looked up from where she was kneeling on the floor. "Yesterday you didn't even know she needed shots. How were you going to make a decision on whether or not I chose the right doctor?"

Winston tugged free and went back to playing GI Joe with Bruce and Alec, one sleeve of his jacket dangling behind him.

Liz held up her hand and Griff took it, helping her up with a tug that was anything but gentle. "I'm talking about the appointment, not the doctor."

She brushed off her knees. Cookie crumbs sprinkled back onto the carpet. Time to vacuum again. "Can't you get time off from work?"

"Yes, I can, but—"

"But what?" She had a hunch she knew what the problem was, but she wasn't going to make it any easier on him. In her opinion, she had made things just about as easy as she was going to. He had to do a little bridging here if anything was to work between them.

He looked down, contemplating his words. How to ask without making it seem as if he needed her? Damn, it seemed that he needed her more and more for all those little things that concerned Casie. For all the little things that concerned him.

"Come with me." The words were fairly growled out.

"Is that an order?"

"No," he said tersely. "That's a request."

"Well, since you asked so nicely." She patted his cheek. "I wouldn't have dreamed of letting you go alone, anyway."

But Liz had said that the appointment was for early tomorrow morning. She had all these children to take care of. "Do we have to take them?" He gestured around to encompass the roomful of boys.

She grinned. "It might guarantee us faster service, but I think I can prevail on a friend to watch them for tomorrow."

"That must be some friend."

Cries of outrage suddenly rose as Bruce and Alec began rolling around on the floor, both trying to maintain their hold on the object of contention: a baseball glove. Griff took a few steps toward them. Liz watched, curious. He crouched over the boys, a darkly disapproving scowl on his face.

The boys sprang apart immediately without uttering a single word in protest. The glove remained on the floor. Winston dashed by and scooped it up.

"She's not all that altruistic. I take over her kids on occasion when she's strapped. She runs a day care, too. From the looks of it, both of us could take a few lessons from you." She nodded toward the two boys. Both were docilely coloring now, the picture of good manners.

"Discipline is about the only thing I could teach."

"Oh—" she took hold of his shirtfront and ran her hand along it softly, her eyes saying words that she couldn't at the moment "—I don't know about that."

She could summon urges from thin air and make him ache for her just like that, he thought. But then, she had help. His mind had turned on him as well as his body. More and more he began to entertain the idea that perhaps, just perhaps, he could feel, could let himself go. He could cross over into that land that Liz held out to him, a land of love and caring.

At least, it might be worth a try.

"Then you can come with me?"

She bent over to pick Casie up out of the playpen. "Wild horses wouldn't keep me away. Besides, I owe it to Casie." She patted the baby's bottom. Good. Dry.

He picked up his niece's jacket and held it out to Liz. "Care to explain that?"

"If I let you loose with her at the doctor's office, you might punch him out when he makes her cry—and they're all guaranteed to cry during their first encounter with the good doctor. Here. Hold her."

He positioned the baby so that Liz could slip on her jacket. "That's ridiculous. I would not punch him out."

The smug look she gave him told him she knew better.

Maybe she did at that, he thought not altogether grudgingly. Maybe she did know better. About a lot of things.

Chapter Ten

"You're dead!"

"Am not, you are. I got you."

"You can't get anyone when you're dead!"

"MAAAA!"

"I'm so sorry," a dark-haired woman mumbled to Griff as she ushered her two sons away from his chair and to another part of the doctor's waiting room.

"I'm sure she is," Griff said to Liz, eyeing the two towheaded boys. If they were cats, he was certain there would be fur flying right about now.

"Probably, but it has its rewards." Liz looked at him knowingly.

He didn't bother answering. Instead, he went on flipping through the magazine he held. Not a single word registered. She was right. It *did* have its rewards, rewards he had thought he was immune to. He had to admit it. He had undergone a transformation.

Like it or not, he was part of a family unit, he and Casie. And Liz. He was sure that for all intents and purposes, they looked like a typical young family.

Well, not exactly typical, he amended, glancing at Liz on his left. By no stretch of the imagination could Liz be called a typical anything. She had dropped into his life like a bolt of lightning.

Or a lifesaver to grab in the sea of darkness and despair.

She could feel him looking at her. The expression on his face was pensive. Was he worried about what was going to happen once they went behind the door that separated the waiting room from the doctor's office?

"What's on your mind?" She lifted her foot as a little boy, no more than three, ran his truck right by her and kept on going.

"Jonathan, come back here," his mother cried and scooped him up bodily. She flashed Liz an apologetic smile.

The fact that Liz seemed to be able to pick up on his thoughts bothered him. He was a private person. He didn't like anyone rummaging through his mind as if it was an extension of their own. And he didn't want her to know that he was thinking about her.

"Just that I wonder how good an idea this really is, taking Casie to see a doctor when she's well." He watched Liz's face. She looked as if she accepted his answer. Well, why shouldn't she? She couldn't really read his mind, couldn't tell that every second thought seemed to center around her lately. He was letting his imagination run away with him.

His concern about Casie was endearingly sweet, especially since he tried to be so gruff about it. Just another reason to love him. "I agree." Liz nodded knowingly. "Back when we were kids, our moms only took us when we were sick. I guess that's why you look so uncomfortable here. You probably unconsciously associate a lot of fear with being in a doctor's office."

He continued pretending to read the magazine on his lap. "No, I don't." His voice was flat.

"Oh, excuse me." She might have known his male pride wouldn't let him admit to that. "You were never afraid when you went to the doctor." Most likely, the doctor was afraid of seeing you. You probably snapped his head off and questioned his every move.

"No, I never went to the doctor." Casie reached out to him. He let the magazine drop to the floor and took her into his arms.

Now he was claiming to be invincible. Liz remembered all the bouts of cold and flu that had abounded in her household when she was growing up. "I suppose you were never sick?"

"No, I didn't say that. I just never went to the doctor."

She saw his annoyed embarrassment and realized her blunder. *Liz, when will you learn to keep your mouth shut?* "Oh. I'm sorry." She touched his arm to emphasize her point.

Griff's expression softened a little. There was no way she could know anything. He couldn't blame her.

"I didn't mean to pry. There's no shame in your parents not having enough money to afford to take

you to a doctor. You're lucky that you never got seri-
ously ill.''

Gently, he removed Casie's hands from the button
on his shirt that she was trying to pry off. "Let's just
say that the money was more important."

Liz looked at him incredulously. "More important
than you?"

Bingo, he thought wryly.

The inner door to the doctor's office opened a crack
at a time. Two little girls squealed and scurried out of
the way. A young nurse wearing white slacks and a
tunic with a bright yellow happy face pinned to it
peered around the door cautiously, apparently hoping to avoid any unforeseen collisions.

"Casie Foster?" The nurse looked around the
semifilled waiting room.

Griff rose instantly. "That's us."

The wall was back up again, Liz thought as she
stood up next to him. For a moment there, she had
thought she was finally on to something. The nurse's
entrance couldn't have been timed any worse than if
Griff had preordained it.

He might have won temporary reprieve, but she
wasn't going to be put off for long, Liz told herself. He
had raised too many questions in her mind for her to
back off now. Was that why he was so reserved? Because his parents hadn't cared enough about him and
his sister? Had they rejected his love so callously, so
completely, that he felt it was safer not to love at all?
She had to find out. If she didn't, how could she make
him see that it was different with her?

* * *

Bellowing indignantly at the top of her lungs, Casie was pronounced in the pink of health.

"She doesn't like being handled," Griff noted to Liz as Casie cried in reaction to the doctor's thorough exam.

"Seems to run in the family." Liz gave him an innocent grin when he shot her a look.

"Depends on the handler."

Liz's grin grew broader.

To celebrate the successful outing, Griff offered to take them out to eat.

Liz was stunned and pleased by this uncharacteristic gesture. He was really coming out of his reclusive shell, she thought. Her pleasure abated a little when he brought the three of them to eat at a local fast-food restaurant in the mall.

"You really are the last of the big-time spenders," Liz said with a laugh as they picked out the shortest line to stand in.

"To go out to a fancy restaurant, we'd have to leave her with a sitter." He nodded at Casie.

She looked down at the child, who was trying to wiggle out of her stroller. "And you didn't like the idea of leaving her with a stranger," Liz guessed. She laughed. "You certainly have come a long way in the last month, Foster. You were more than willing to leave her with a stranger then."

"You mean you?" She nodded in response. "That was different. I had my back against the wall. I didn't have much of a choice then."

"Next," cried the harried-looking attendant behind the register.

Liz nudged him. "You're on, Foster."

"What do you want?" he asked. He heard the attendant sigh impatiently at this conference.

"A garden salad, diet dressing and a diet soda."

He let his eyes skim over her frame. She was wearing jeans and a pullover. They accentuated her best features just as well as the beaded gown had. The word *perfect* came to mind.

"Diet? You get any thinner and you'll waste away."

"If I don't watch my body, you won't." Her eyes laughed gaily.

"You two gonna order or make eyes at each other?" the attendant wanted to know.

"I don't know," Liz murmured, still looking at Griff, "how much does the second choice cost?"

She was really something else, Griff thought. This time the assessment was made with a growing warm glow of pleasure.

"Lady, there're people waiting behind you." The teenager jabbed a bony finger impatiently into the air, pointing behind her.

She flashed the teenager a smile and turned to Griff. "I'll stake out a table and let you handle this."

"That's a first. Hey—" Griff swung around "—what do I get for the kid?" he called after Liz.

"Get her some French fries. She'll have fun squeezing them," Liz answered as she threaded her way through the crowd.

Dragging a high chair with a clown face on the tray in her wake, Liz finally found a table near the entrance for the three of them.

It took Griff several minutes to find them.

"If you were any farther out, you'd be sitting in the middle of the mall," he complained as he deposited the tray on the table.

"Look, finding a table today is no mean feat. In case you haven't noticed, this place is absolutely crawling with last-minute Christmas shoppers." She circled her hand in the air and hit a passerby. The woman gave her a cold look. "Sorry." Liz let her hand drop.

Griff didn't bother trying to hide his grin. "Why not try using just your mouth and not your whole body when you talk?"

He placed the paper container of French fries on Casie's tray. She immediately turned it upside down and seemed to take great glee in watching the shower of fries hit the tray, table and floor.

"Speaking of Christmas," Liz began as she bent down and picked up the fries closest to her, "what are you planning to do about it?"

Griff poked a hole in the plastic cover on his soda. "They won't let me abolish it, so I guess it'll go on as usual."

"You know what I mean."

"Liz, don't give me that much credit. I *never* know what you mean." Not waiting for her to answer, he unwrapped his hamburger and began to eat.

She wondered if he was just goading her. "This is Casie's first Christmas and I just wondered what you were going to do."

He shrugged. "I hadn't planned on anything."

She stared at him. "Hadn't planned on—? Haven't you gotten a tree?"

"No tree."

Liz's mouth dropped open. How could he not have a tree? Even he couldn't be that insensitive. "You can't be serious."

Griff raised his eyes and looked at her for a long moment. "Why?"

"Why?" she echoed incredulously. "It's practically her birthright to have a Christmas tree. Didn't *you* have a tree every Christmas?"

"No, I didn't." Granted, he was taking liberties with her question. There had been Christmas trees in some of the houses he had stayed in. But they had been for the foster parents' children, never for him. And the families he had stayed with had never made him feel as if he was anything but an outsider.

For a moment, she hesitated. The look in his eyes warned her to stop. But her overwhelming need to know about him pushed her on. He couldn't keep locking doors every time she knocked. "I want to know," she said softly. "Now."

He dropped the hamburger on the tray, his appetite gone. "Know what?"

"About you." Liz put her hand over his. "About your childhood." He pulled his hand back and she tried not to show him how much that hurt.

"I didn't have one."

"Meaning?"

"Meaning I didn't have Christmases or birthdays, or toys. Just beatings, endless chores and a parade of strangers the orphanage found to take Sally and me in for money."

"You didn't have any parents?" she asked in a hushed voice.

The laugh he uttered was bitter. "Not even when we lived with them. Not in the sense you mean. My father was too drunk and my mother too frightened of him and of living to keep us." Anger rose in his eyes. "Satisfied?"

She shook her head slowly, fighting back the tears at the images that his words evoked. Now she understood. Everything. "No. Not until I can give you both your first Christmas."

"Look, Christmas is for children...."

He didn't want her pity. He didn't know what had possessed him to tell her all of that just now. Maybe it was a need to open up, just this once, to expose to sunshine the wounds he always carried with him. Maybe then they would finally heal. And she was sunshine. But right now he cursed her for it, for making him so vulnerable, for stripping him of his shield.

She saw the look in his eyes. He was withdrawing again. She'd be damned if she'd let him this time. "And we're all children at bottom."

"Some more so than others." His meaning was clear. He meant to hurt her because she, with her probing, had hurt him, had made him hurt again. The memories always accomplished that.

She leaned over and wiped a tiny dot of ketchup from the corner of his mouth. "No argument," she said with forced brightness. "Now finish eating, we've got a lot of shopping to do."

He was grateful the subject was dropped. But he didn't like the topic it was exchanged for. "Now?" He looked around. "Liz, there are hundreds of people around."

"Maybe thousands. That's what makes it fun." She snapped the lid back down on her unfinished salad. "You've got to be introduced the right way." She curled her fingers around his hand and pulled him to his feet. "C'mon, you've got a lot of catching up to do."

"I don't suppose that telling you that I don't want to catch up would do any good."

She took Casie out of the high chair and placed her in the stroller. "Not in the slightest."

"I didn't think so."

He knew he should protest harder, that if he put his foot down, she'd have to listen. But he didn't want her to listen. He needed to be forced. He couldn't do it on his own. He wanted her to pull him into that crazy fantasy world that always seemed to surround her. Just this one time.

For the next three hours, she indoctrinated him just as she had promised. She dragged him from store to store, sometimes to buy something, sometimes just to "sample the ambience." With effort, they snaked their way through the walls of pressing bodies and harried shoppers. The toy stores were particularly crowded and represented a real challenge. But they managed. And throughout it all, though he'd never admit it to her verbally, he was enjoying himself.

"Now what?" he groaned when she pulled him over to a long, winding line in the center of the mall. The carousel with its horses stood dormant, in silent deference to the oversize, white-haired, round-bellied elf in crimson who was sitting before a camera and having his picture taken with an endless procession of children.

"Now," Liz announced, "Casie gets to have her picture taken with Santa Claus."

"She doesn't even know who Santa Claus is," Griff protested.

He was tired, and his arms ached from the packages he was carrying. But his words weren't delivered as forcefully as they might have been. She was right about this. She was right about everything. He found himself enjoying this noisy madness, enjoying having someone to do it for. To share it with. The years of solitude he had spent had been filled with only emptiness. He felt full now. And happy.

Liz listened to his protest the way she seemed to listen to everything else he said, he observed. Not at all.

"She will eventually," Liz assured him soothingly, "and then she can look back at this picture. It'll give her memories."

"She's too young for memories."

Liz nudged him to move up as the line snaked its way forward another foot. "No one's too young to start having memories."

She was right about that, too. His memories were filled with fear and pain and rejection. He didn't want that for Casie. Or himself any longer.

But the line *was* awfully long.

"Maybe we can come back tomorrow," he suggested.

Liz stood firm. "Don't try to weasel out of this, Foster. Tomorrow is Christmas Eve. It'll be even more packed than this. Besides, you still have a tree to buy and decorate."

He groaned. "C'mon, Liz, there isn't enough time for all that."

She ignored his appeal. "There is if you work it right. We'll pick out a tree after this and I have a wonderful box of ornaments I can give you. Hand painted. They were my grandmother's." They gained another few inches on the line.

"Why aren't *you* using them?" he asked suspiciously.

"I am. She believed in a very big tree and she was always making decorations for the family and herself. Thirty years' worth of decorations adds up to quite a lot of decorations."

A performer, dressed as Humpty Dumpty, danced by to entertain the children. He stopped to hand Casie a candy cane made out of red and white pipe cleaners, tipped his hat to Liz and scampered on.

"I've always felt bad that her decorations couldn't all be fully appreciated." Liz took the "candy cane" away from Casie just as she tried to pop it into her mouth. "I know Grandma would have loved you to have them."

Griff tapped her on the shoulder and pointed to the gap that had been formed in front of them. Liz moved the stroller up. "What makes you think that?"

Liz grinned up at him. "She adored stubborn cops with silky mustaches that tickle."

He loved seeing laughter in her eyes. And yes, he admitted to himself, he loved *her*.

Giving in to the sudden impulse that overtook him, Griff leaned over, cupped her chin in his hand and kissed her, right there in the middle of the mall, on line to see Santa Claus.

Liz felt her heart beating in her throat as she looked at him in stunned surprise. He couldn't have given her a better gift if he had presented her with a diamond necklace.

She touched his lips, a smile playing on her own. "To be continued," she whispered. "After the tree-trimming party."

"You're planning on a party?"

"A very intimate party of two."

He was beginning to like some of her plans.

It took them a full hour to finally get up to the front of the line.

"This better be worth it," Griff muttered as they took their place at the head of the ramp.

A white-haired woman dressed in a ruffled red-checkered apron that touched the floor stood before them. Mrs. Claus. She watched the child in front of them squirm on Santa's lap and cry as an attendant set up the photograph.

"Dickens must have had you in mind when he wrote *A Christmas Carol*," Liz told Griff.

The child ahead of them was finished. "Just the one?" asked Mrs. Claus.

"Yes." Liz took Casie out of her stroller and smoothed down her wispy hair. She turned to look at Griff. "No."

"No?" Griff looked around. Now what was she talking about?

He found out when Liz grabbed his hand and pulled him up the ramp to Santa's domain with her.

"We'd like to be in on it, too, please," she told the person wearing green tights, green livery and an elf's hat. The man, positioned behind the camera, straightened and looked over to Mrs. Claus for instructions. The short, squat woman raised her shoulders up and down.

"It's rather unusual." Her tiny rosebud mouth pointed down.

Santa came to Liz's rescue. Somehow, Griff thought, he might have known it would go this way. "Oh, it's Christmas," Santa said with a hearty laugh, gesturing them forward.

"Yes," Liz said, looking over at Griff, "it is." Griff scowled at her but she was sure he did it just for effect. Placing Casie on Santa's lap, Liz leaned back against one of the chair's arms and motioned for Griff to do the same on the other. Grudgingly, he did.

"Sorry my lap isn't big enough for all of you." Santa chuckled.

"That's okay. Just don't forget to leave something special under the tree. Once we get it." Liz leaned over and looked meaningfully at Griff.

She had storm trooped into his life and he only had himself to blame.

And thank.

The feeling dissipated somewhat as he followed Liz from tree to tree in a lot just off the main thoroughfare in Bedford.

"Liz, any tree'll do!" he insisted. Casie began to protest loudly and he shifted her to his other shoulder. "How about this one?"

She looked at the one he pointed to and then gave him a dubious look. "Too scrawny."

"Liz, I'm only keeping it for a few days. I'm not planning on marrying it."

She ignored him and continued looking.

The weary-looking owner of the lot rubbed his hands together. The weather was turning unseasonably cold. "Lady, this is almost Christmas Eve. The perfect ones are gone." Getting nowhere with Liz, he turned to Griff. "Is your wife always this picky?" he asked Griff.

"No, usually she's worse," Griff answered. He opened his mouth to correct the lot owner's mistaken impression of their relationship, but never got the chance.

"How about this one?" the man asked, leading Liz to the other end of the lot.

Liz circled it slowly, studying it from all angles. This one was more to her liking. Not without reservations, but it would do.

"Okay."

"Hallelujah," the owner mumbled into his triple chins. He and Griff quickly did the monetary exchange and strapped the tree onto the roof of Griff's car before Liz could change her mind.

"Pretty proud of yourself, aren't you?" Griff asked Liz as they drove back home.

She turned to look at him. The harsh lines she had come to know had softened around his mouth and eyes. She was getting to him and she knew it. "Yeah, I am."

He read the knowing look on her face. "Just for that, I should make you walk home."

"You do and you'll never get my grandmother's decorations."

"The one who liked cops."

"The one who liked cops. Did I tell you that that trait is genetically transferred?"

They stopped for a light. He ran his hand along her cheek, pushing aside a strand of blond hair. "That's possibly the only thing you didn't tell me. Did the other members of your family ever get to say anything while you lived at home?"

"Sure. Usually 'Yes, Liz.'"

"I thought as much."

He laughed. It filled the car and her heart. It was going to be one hell of a Christmas, she promised herself.

Chapter Eleven

Happiness.

Was that what this alien sensation was? He wasn't altogether certain. Happiness was something that had continually eluded him all the years he was growing up and all the years of his manhood. But if he had to put a name to the feeling that bubbled and surged through him now, that would be his guess. Happiness. Nothing else could feel quite this way, make him quite this...hopeful. What was happening in his life at this time was good, it was right. With this feeling rushing through his veins, he felt confident enough to take a chance, just this one more time, and let himself go all the way. The rewards could be so great. He had always been afraid of failing. The pain of failure was always there, waiting to seize him. The threat of it had always outweighed everything else. But Liz had changed all that, had changed him. She had made him want to try again.

Casie babbled at him from her car seat, playing with a chewable, squeaky toy Liz had given her before he dropped her off. He felt more relaxed and at peace than he ever had before.

"So what do you think, Casie?" He tilted the rearview mirror to catch a glimpse of the baby. "You think we might make a real family, the three of us?"

"Mfghp."

"I'll take that as a yes."

Sally wasn't coming back. He had combed the county for her on his own and pulled in a few favors he had coming to him from other officers in the region. It had all been strictly off the record. They all had the same thing to report. Sally was nowhere to be found. And, Griff was beginning to realize, she might not be for years to come. He had Casie to think of. And his own life.

They could be a family. It would work. He'd make it work.

"Maybe Liz has something. Maybe sometimes dreams can come true."

"Ayhfee."

"Right again, kid."

He turned the car onto his cul-de-sac. Everything within him froze.

It was like experiencing déjà vu. Sally was standing on his doorstep.

And she wasn't alone. But this time, it wasn't a baby she had brought with her.

Griff pulled in a deep breath, trying to fortify himself. Next to Sally stood a tall, gangly man with long dark hair that swept the top of his shoulders. His hands were defiantly shoved into the pockets of his plaid wool jacket.

At least his hair looked clean this time, Griff noted bitterly.

Griff felt a sudden surge of anger that shattered the delicate, spun-glass world he had been building just a moment before. Sally had brought Buddy with her. Casie's father.

Her *biological* father, Griff reminded himself. Anyone could sire a child. It took almost no trouble at all. That didn't give the man any rights.

Griff slowly pulled his car into the driveway and parked it next to a maroon van that had a large dent on the right side. His, no doubt.

"Griff!" Sally came running up to his car before he had a chance to get out.

Buddy remained standing on the front step, warily watching the scene unfold. Griff hardly spared him more than a glance.

"There she is! There's my baby!" Sally hastily, undid Casie's straps. "Oh, Casie, I've missed you so!" Casie whimpered uncertainly.

"She hardly knows you," Griff said, getting out. "They tend to forget quickly at her age." He took Casie from her. "At yours, too."

Sally's expression faded to one of confusion. She pushed her hair out of her eyes. "Griff, I had to get some things cleared up. You know that."

"What I know is that you left her behind like so much excess baggage," he accused. He saw Sally's eyes widen in disbelief. He had always been there to pick up the pieces for her, to cover for her when she needed it. This was something new.

"Griff, that's not fair," Sally cried. But she made no move to take Casie back.

He struggled with his anger. And with feeling threatened. "What isn't fair is to come waltzing in and out of people's lives like some carefree child without any responsibilities."

Tears gathered in Sally's eyes. Griff looked away. The sight of her pain hurt him. But if he gave in, he'd lose Casie, lose something precious, something he had just found for himself. He had to stand firm, even if it was against Sally.

Even if it was wrong.

"I know, Griff, I know." Sally touched his arm. He stiffened.

"If you know that, what are you doing here?"

In answer Sally turned behind her and held out her hand to Buddy.

"What? Him? What's he got to do with it?"

Buddy crossed over to Sally. He took her hand and for the first time, looked directly at Griff. Only the slight movement at the corner of his mouth showed his nervousness. "We're married now, Griff," Buddy said. He held up their joined hands. There was a wedding ring on both.

The news stunned Griff, but it didn't alter anything. Buddy had walked out once. What was there to change that now? "Married, huh? For how long?"

"Forever," Sally answered defiantly.

"Terrific." His angry gaze swept over both of them, measuring them. They came up wanting. "Two people who turn tail and run whenever the going gets rough. Where does that leave Casie?" he demanded.

Oblivious to the emotional turmoil around her, Casie settled down and began to play with the buttons on Griff's jacket.

"With her parents. With two people who love her," Sally insisted.

The look in her eyes told Griff that she was afraid, really afraid of him, of what he might do. He felt a stab of pain that things should come to this between them. She had never been afraid of him. But he had never had Casie to think of before.

"She has that now. I can give her what she needs. A home, love."

Buddy stepped forward, an obvious angry retort on his lips. Sally put her hand out to stop him. "Griff, please," she implored her brother. "Listen to me."

He wanted to go. To shut the door in their faces, to turn his back on this threat to the little bit of happiness he had finally uncovered for himself.

But she was his sister, and he loved her. He couldn't win his own happiness at the cost of hers. And Casie was hers.

He turned up the collar on Casie's jacket. The wind had picked up again. There was the taste of winter in the air. "Let's go into the house before she comes down with something."

Sally reached for Casie. Griff pretended he didn't notice. He kept the baby close to him as he unlocked the front door. The Christmas tree on the roof of his car was forgotten. Everything was forgotten except for the drama that was being played out in front of him.

Walking in, he turned on the light. Nothing could bring back the light to his soul. He held Casie tighter. An ache began to grow. A deep, foreboding dread. Casie complained and he loosened his hold.

"Well?"

Sally and Buddy stood before him, their hands joined. He felt like some sort of a horrid ogre, threatening two frightened young people. But, damn it, they were threatening *him*. They couldn't just deposit a human being on him, let him learn to love her, and then whisk her away again. It wasn't fair, damn it!

When had life ever been fair?

A deep, dark bleakness seized him in a viselike grip. At that moment, he knew he had lost.

"I'm listening," he said to Sally quietly.

"We're married," Sally said nervously.

"You already said that."

"And Buddy has a job."

"Where?" He turned to look at Buddy, not bothering to mask his contempt. Buddy had never been able to hold on to a job for more than a couple of days. All he had ever cared about was playing his guitar and riding his motorcycle. "In a band?"

"No," Sally cried. "In a bank."

Griff saw the pride on her face as she looked at the man beside her. "Working, or making withdrawals?" Griff's implication was clear.

"Working," Buddy retorted. "And I'm going to school at night. I've got my head together."

"About time," Griff said dryly.

His hold was slipping. He knew that he could fight them for Casie's custody. And there were chances that he might even win. But *what* would he win? Sally's tears? Her hatred? A little girl who would ask questions about her mother when she grew older? Who might hate him too for perpetuating this schism? It was too selfish a move, no matter how much he wanted it.

"Where do you plan on living?"

"We've got an apartment in Tustin. It's not too far from here. You can come by and see her any time you want," Sally said eagerly. She began to ease Casie back into her arms.

She always knew when she was winning, Griff thought. He let Casie go. "Count on it."

"Oh, Griff, thank you." Sally threw one arm around him as she held Casie with the other. "I don't know what I would have done without you."

"Yeah, me neither," he muttered.

Sally drew back and turned toward Buddy. Griff watched the expression on Buddy's face as he took his daughter's small hand in his. There was affection there. Maybe it would work. If not, he'd be there to take her back. "What's the name of the bank?" he asked Buddy.

Buddy looked up from his daughter. "First National Trust on Newport and Third."

"I'll be by to check it out," Griff promised. There was no mistaking the message.

"Do that. Open an account. We could always use the business." The lopsided grin on the thin face was uncertain, but hopeful.

There was no use in biting off his brother-in-law's head. It wouldn't help erase the pain that was chewing up his gut. The awful, gnawing pain that began to consume him even as he stood there. He wanted them gone. He wanted to be alone, as he always had been. "It's past her bedtime. You'd better get her home."

Sally nodded. She stood on her toes and gave Griff a quick kiss on the cheek.

He scarcely felt it. He scarcely felt anything. It should have remained that way from the beginning, he told himself. He should never have been so stupid as to let Liz stir up his feelings and make him care. It was all her fault. And his.

"She's got a bunch of things here." He gestured around the room vaguely.

"We can come by and pick them up after the holidays." Sally was fairly beaming. "We've got all she'll need in the car."

"In the car?" Griff repeated, puzzled.

"We're spending Christmas with Buddy's folks in Santa Barbara. They're excited about seeing the baby." Her voice lowered. "Thank you, Griff. Thank you so much for everything."

Buddy offered him his hand and there was nothing Griff could do but shake it. At least Sally was happy, he thought. "Take care of them both, or you'll answer to me."

"I already know that," Buddy said with a nervous laugh.

And then they were gone.

And so was everything else.

Griff turned out the light and sat down in the living room. He hadn't even bothered taking off his jacket. It had all happened so fast. As he leaned back against the sofa, something stiff rose up in his pocket. He tugged it out impatiently without thinking.

It was a copy of the photograph they had had taken this afternoon. Griff stared at it for a moment. It seemed to have all happened in another lifetime now. He crumpled it and let it fall to the floor.

There were no lights coming from Griff's house as Liz drove up. Fear erupted and began to grow. What was wrong? He had to be home, his car was in the driveway. The tree was still strapped to the roof.

Casie!

Something had happened to Casie. Liz brought the car to a screeching halt and jumped out. The car began to roll backward. Swearing under her breath, Liz quickly hopped in and pulled up the hand brake. The car jarred to a halt. Leaving the car door hanging wide open, she ran up to Griff's front door and rang the bell. When there was no answer, she began pounding on the door.

"Griff, it's me, Liz! Griff, are you in there? Open up!"

She continued pounding. The side of her closed fist was beginning to ache when the door was suddenly pulled open.

She gasped when she saw him. He didn't look like the same man she had been with only half an hour ago.

He looked dark, foreboding. It *was* Casie. Something awful had happened, she could feel it.

"Where's Casie?" She began to dash toward the back of the house.

"She's gone."

The words were cold, still. With a feeling of absolute dread, Liz swung around to face him. "What do you mean, gone?"

"Sally came back."

She couldn't believe it. "And she took the baby? Just like that?"

"Looks that way."

The bitterness in his voice was so strong it was almost visible. She knew how much he had come to care for Casie, how much he loved her. That he did was a hard-won breakthrough, one that affected them both. Liz ached for him, but didn't know what to say.

Instinctively, she reached out and put her arms around him. Griff tried to brush her aside. Liz wouldn't let him. "You're not going to push me away, Griff!" She kept her own hurt out of her voice. Why couldn't he let her in? Why? "I licked a bully when I was eleven and I know how to hang on. You're not retreating from me again—"

"Liz, there's no use—"

"There's *every* use," she insisted. She struggled to maintain her composure and keep her tears back. He wasn't going to shut her out again, he *wasn't*. "Where did Sally take Casie?"

Pushing her arms aside, he moved away from her and stood by the window, staring out blankly. "They're going to visit his parents in Santa Barbara."

She watched the set of his shoulders, the way he moved. She was losing him. "They?"

"He married her. That would-be rock star who ran out on her." He spat the words out. "He changed his mind and came back. He's working at a bank now."

Liz pressed her lips together, searching for words. "Well, that sounds hopeful."

He turned to look at her. She could almost touch the anger in his eyes. "Yeah, just dandy."

Please don't do this, she thought. "Are they going to live in Santa Barbara?"

"No. Tustin."

Liz grabbed the small bit of good news and clung to it for all it was worth. "Then we can see her. Casie, I mean."

"We?"

Why was he saying it as if it were some sort of foreign word? As if he hadn't held her, kissed her? As if their souls hadn't touched? "Yes, 'we.' I love her too, Griff."

"I never said I love her," he retorted. To love was to hurt. He wasn't going to hurt anymore. Nothing mattered. Nothing.

"You didn't have to."

He wanted her to go, to go before he broke down. "Maybe you'd better go home."

She swallowed, pulling her courage to her. "All right, after we decorate the tree."

She had to get him moving, had to get through to him somehow. If she didn't do it now, she'd lose forever. "You have a tree strapped to the roof of your car that's going to turn brown if you don't put it in water."

"Take it home."

"I already have a tree."

"Have two," he said bitterly. He had let her convince him that dreams were possible. He had *believed*. He had been an idiot. Nothing ever changed. Not for him. "Give one to that friend of yours. What's-his-name." He waved his hand impatiently. "Vinnie."

"Vinnie has his own tree. He doesn't need another. You do," she insisted.

"I don't need anything." He clenched his fists as he shouted. "Now will you just get out of here and leave me alone?"

She wanted to lash out at him, to scream at him and tell him what a fool he was for turning his back on what they had, but she knew that wouldn't do any good. He wouldn't hear her. He had shut her out completely.

"All right." Liz mustered all the dignity she could. "I'll leave the decorations on the doorstep in case you change your mind."

"I won't change my mind." His face was dark and expressionless again as he struggled to regain control.

She raised her chin up high. "Then, Officer Foster, you're a bigger damn fool than I thought you were."

She saw the crumpled photograph on the floor. Stooping down, she picked it up and looked at it. She barely saw it through her tears. Silently, she put it in her purse and walked out.

He heard the door slam hard.

She left him standing in the dark. In more ways than one.

Chapter Twelve

Damn him, where *was* he?

Liz moved restlessly around her living room, picking up different Christmas knickknacks, adjusting them and then putting them down again. She had no idea what she was handling.

For possibly what felt like the hundredth time that day, she went to the window by the front door, pushed aside the curtain and looked out. He wasn't anywhere in sight. Liz let the filmy curtain fall from her hand.

He wasn't coming. Why was she doing this to herself? The man just didn't care.

She missed him, missed him terribly. Missed seeing him trudge up her walk with Casie in his arms. It was only one day and yet she felt as if she were going through a whole agonizing spectrum of pain. She ran her hands along her arms. Was *he* suffering like this?

She no longer felt as though she had any answers, especially when it came to what Griff felt.

Could he just drop out of her life like this without a word? Without even goodbye? Didn't he feel anything? Was it only her? Had she only been fooling herself all this time?

No, it wasn't one-sided. It *wasn't*. He was just being pigheaded and stupid.

So what else was new?

She ached. Everything inside felt twisted, lost, empty. It wasn't right that she should feel this way on Christmas Eve, so alone, so deserted.

This was the way *he* had felt when he was a boy, Liz thought with a sudden pang. But she wanted to fill that void for him, to erase some of that loneliness from his soul. *He* was the one who wouldn't let her.

Damn him and his male pride.

Her eyes misted again. She swung around, searching for a tissue, and knocking over a heralding angel that was standing next to the manger. Wiping her eyes with the back of her hand, she bent over to pick up the broken figure from the floor. The angel was permanently separated from his trumpet.

Liz put the two pieces aside on the coffee table. She'd fix the statue later. Much later. Right now, she couldn't quite seem to function. She had no idea how she had managed to get through the day. She remembered only bits and pieces of it. Her group of charges were even more rambunctious than usual, excitedly anticipating Christmas and a cache of presents. The boys had all wanted to know what had happened to Casie and why she wasn't there. Alec had even drawn a picture for her as a gift and had painstakingly wrapped it. He had been disappointed that Casie wasn't there to receive it. Liz had tried to tell them as best as possible without crying.

She had even conjured up a festive facade from somewhere and played games with the boys and sang Christmas carols. The hardest part had been going through the motions of a Christmas play she had put together in the past two weeks. Casie was to have played Baby Jesus. A doll was found to take her place. None of the parents who attended the performances had noticed that there was anything wrong.

Only Liz knew that things would never be right again.

Wandering around, she accidentally kicked over the suitcase she had packed last night. Righting it, she ran her fingers over the handle. She had told herself that she would leave for her parents' house right after the boys had been picked up. But that had been hours ago. She had procrastinated, waiting, long after the last boy, Winston, had gone, candy cane in hand, yelling out, "Merry Christmas, Whiz!" Waiting for Griff to come, to call.

But he hadn't.

"No, Virginia, there is no Santa Claus," she murmured looking at the clock.

Six-thirty.

He got off work at five. He was probably home. Maybe if she—

No, darn it. No. All the overt moves had been hers. She had tried, tried her hardest to show him the way, to bridge that gap between him and the rest of the world. She had put on her seven-league boots and met him three quarters of the way. If he didn't come to her on his own, it wouldn't be any good.

It wasn't any good now, either.

She reshuffled the figures that were arranged around the manger, closing the ranks now that the angel had abruptly departed.

The doorbell rang and she dropped a shepherd.

Her heart hammering in her throat, she ran up to the door and swung it open. A moment later, she felt the light go out of her soul.

"Oh, hi, Vinnie." She took a step back. "Come on inside."

Vinnie walked in, opening two buttons on his long black coat and loosening his white silk scarf. He eyed her curiously. "I've heard more enthusiastic greetings given to investigating IRS agents."

"Sorry." Forcing her mind to function, she realized that he was dressed formally. "Did I forget that we were going somewhere?"

She hoped not. She wasn't in the mood to go anywhere there were crowds of people and cheery voices. Not tonight. Her mind had been in a total fog ever since she had left Griff's house. She had lain awake all night waiting for him to call, fighting the temptation to pick up the phone herself. She didn't think she could go on pretending to be happy any longer. She had given her all to the children and she felt utterly drained.

"No. I just dropped by to wish you a Merry Christmas and to give you this." Vinnie handed her a small box wrapped in white tissue paper. There was a dark blue bow with streamers attached to it. "I know what a sucker you are for that type of thing—" he nodded at the box "—although it really has no musically redeeming value."

She stared at the gift in her hand for a minute, then came to. "Oh, I have one for you, too, under the tree." It was a sweater she had picked out in his favorite colors.

It took her a few minutes to find it even though she had put the gaily wrapped box beneath the tree in the past half hour. It was, she realized, as if her soul was shell-shocked. She had hoped too much and had been disappointed. Was this the way Griff had always felt?

Oh, God, Griff, how awful.

When she didn't turn around, Vinnie tapped her on the shoulder. "Would you like to go out with me tonight?" he asked gently, his voice full of understanding.

She turned around, the first tears she had ever let him see shimmering in her eyes. "I'd make a terrible date tonight. Here." She thrust the present toward him in an effort to change the subject.

"Thanks." He pulled out a handkerchief from his breast pocket and handed it to her. "You could never make a terrible date." He watched as she dabbed at her eyes. "You want to talk about it?"

"No."

"This is even worse than I thought." He tucked his gift under his arm. "Come with me, Liz. They're playing Handel's *Messiah*. It'll perk you up. I can get you an extra ticket at the box office. I've actually got a date for tonight, but we can make it a threesome."

She almost said yes, but then she shook her head. "No, I feel like being by myself. You go ahead and enjoy yourself."

He shrugged, shaking his head, obviously not pleased. "Whatever you want, Liz." He pushed the handkerchief back into his pocket. "But if you ask me, he doesn't deserve you."

She kissed his cheek. "You're very sweet."

Vinnie opened the door and then turned around again. "I know." He grinned. "Say hi to your family for me tomorrow." He moved forward and kissed her cheek. "Merry Christmas, friend."

"Merry Christmas, Vinnie."

Liz closed the door and crossed back to the coffee table. Bending down, she picked up the shepherd she had dropped when Vinnie had rung the doorbell. The shepherd's head had fallen off.

"At this rate, there won't be anyone left at the manger by Christmas morning."

She tried to rouse herself by unwrapping Vinnie's present. It was a collection of Christmas carols, sung by different artists, on a compact disc.

"No musically redeeming value." She repeated his words and shook her head.

Trust Vinnie to get in a review even about his. She placed the CD into the stereo set she had in the corner of the room. Familiar voices soon filled the room, singing about the joys of Christmas. Liz waited for herself to be carried away the way she usually was.

She wasn't.

Nothing seemed to help.

There wasn't anything left to do but go to bed and get an early start in the morning, she thought unhappily. Getting down on her knees, she was about to unplug the Christmas lights on the tree when she heard the doorbell again. Liz inched her way back out slowly, careful not to overturn the tree. The way her luck was running, that would be next.

The doorbell rang again, more insistently this time. Someone was leaning on the bell.

Vinnie had probably returned to make one last pitch to get her to go with him, she thought, crossing to the door. He really did have a good heart. Maybe it was time he paid another call to her cousin Rose. Rose would be just about the right age for him now.

You can't even handle your own affairs, what right have you to play matchmaker for anyone else?

She swung open the door. "Vinnie, I really can't go with you—"

"It's not Vinnie."

She raised her eyes to look at him. Griff stood on her doorstep, his suede jacket hanging open, a wary, hopeful, yet hesitant look on his drawn face. "No," she whispered, afraid to believe he was actually here. "It's not."

"Can I come in?" he asked. "You've got every right to say no, but I'd really like to come in. I don't want to be alone tonight."

She came to and realized that she was blocking the doorway. Liz stepped aside and gestured toward the living room. "Sure. Why not? There's lots of room." Her voice sounded high and tinny to her ear. It probably had to do with the sudden, huge knot in her stomach.

He walked in, feeling awkward and uncertain. Like a fumbling boy again, he thought.

"I didn't know whether you'd still be here." He was afraid to look into her eyes, afraid to see rejection there. Instead, he looked around the room. He saw the broken figures on the coffee table and wondered about them. "I thought you might have already left for your mother's. You said you did for the holidays." The words were coming hard and tripped over each other. He wasn't any good at this. But he wasn't any good alone anymore, either.

"I'm leaving in the morning. See," she said, pointing to the suitcase in the corner, "packed and ready." Her hands felt damp. She rubbed her palms on her jeans.

"Yeah." He let out a long sigh. "Am I keeping you from something?"

"No. I was just about to go to bed." She felt edgy, anxious, afraid to hope, afraid not to.

"But you said something about not going with Vinnie when you opened the door—"

"He was by here earlier. He wanted to take me to see Handel's *Messiah*." To keep her hands busy, she picked up the blue ribbon that had been on Vinnie's gift. As she spoke, she wound one of the long, thin streamers around her finger.

"I thought you liked that sort of thing."

"I do."

He watched as she toyed with the ribbon. Was she as nervous as he was? Why? She was the one with all the answers. "Then why didn't you go?"

"I, um, wanted to be alone tonight." She looked away. "I didn't much feel like celebrating."

"Neither did I." He watched as she kept winding the ribbon around. "Do you realize that your finger's turning blue?"

She looked down. He was right. She had wound the ribbon around her finger tightly without realizing it. It wouldn't unwind when she tried to work it free. The ribbon had somehow gotten tangled. She yanked at it and managed only to make it squeeze her finger harder.

"Here, let me." He took her finger and freed it in short order, grateful for somewhere to look besides her eyes. There was so much hurt there.

"Thanks." Liz massaged her throbbing finger, feeling like an idiot. She snatched back a fragment of their conversation to divert his attention. "You never feel like celebrating."

"I have." He wanted to take her in his arms, to hold her, but he knew that he didn't have the right. Not yet. "Lately." He dropped the crumpled ribbon on the coffee table.

She raised her eyes to his face slowly. "You didn't sound like it yesterday."

"Yesterday Sally took Casie away."

"But not forever." Her voice rose, swelled by anger. "You can still see Casie. You can still love her." Hurt feelings came to the surface, demanding restitution. She couldn't hold them back any longer. She had nothing to lose anymore. "You pushed me away. There was no reason for you to treat me the way you did."

"Yes, there was," he told her quietly.

"What?" she cried. "What possible reason could there have been?"

"You opened a door inside me I couldn't shut anymore. Having Sally appear and take Casie back so suddenly made me remember that everything I ever held close was always being taken away from me. And you would go away too, after I had grown to need you." He put his hands on her shoulders, not trusting himself to hold her just yet. "I couldn't run away from you anymore, so I wanted you to run away from me, on my terms. That way it wasn't supposed to hurt. But it's too late for that."

"What are you saying?"

She needed words, more words. She was afraid to take what he had given her and run, afraid that she was writing her own meaning into it.

He wanted to sift her hair through his fingers, to bury his face in it and lose himself in her scent. To be reborn.

"That I had managed to successfuly dam up my feelings until I thought that I didn't need anyone or anything. I did such a good job, I even fooled myself." He touched her face gently, stirring the embers within them both. "And then you came, barging your way into my life—"

"I beg your pardon. Who did the barging?" Tears formed again, but this time she didn't wipe them back. They were tears of joy.

He grinned. "For once, you're going to let me finish a sentence. And then you came," he repeated, growing serious, "and I realized that nothing had changed, not really. Outside, I looked like I was in control, I was strong. But inside—" His voice softened as he looked into her eyes, seeing his own reflection there, seeing his own soul. "Inside there was still this vulnerable little boy who just wanted someone to love him back."

Without hesitation, she put her arms around him. "Oh, Griff, I do."

"I know." Cupping her head with his hand, he stroked her neck with his thumb. "That's why I'm here. Because I know you love me. Because I love you. And because I can't face my first Christmas without you. You promised me Christmas, you know."

She nodded her head. The lump in her throat was so huge she didn't know how she managed to get any words out. "I know."

"My tree still needs trimming."

"Is it still strapped to the roof of your car?" she said, half laughing, half crying.

"No. I took it in this morning, along with your grandmother's decorations."

She disengaged herself suddenly and ran to the closet. Griff watched her, puzzled.

"Where are you going?"

Liz pulled her jacket out of the closet and began putting it on, jamming her arm into the sleeve. "Well, we'd better get to it if we're going to have the tree decorated before we leave." Hurriedly, she pulled on the other sleeve.

"Leave?"

"For my parents' house in the morning. I invited you, remember?"

He grabbed her arm as she hurried to the door.

"What?" she asked as she spun around to face him. Had he suddenly had a change of heart again?

Griff pointed up to the ceiling. "I don't have much experience at this, but I assume that because that shriveled green thing is hanging from the ceiling, it's a mistletoe."

She looked up. "Don't make fun of my mistletoe."

"I'd never make fun of anything that was yours. Does standing under it mean I get to kiss you?" He slipped his hands beneath her jacket and sweater and rested them on the bare skin around her waist. She felt so soft, so inviting. He had lain awake last night thinking of nothing else but her.

She shivered, her eyes never leaving his. "For as long as you want."

"How does forever sound?"

Liz rose on her toes to meet his lips. "It sounds very, very good."

He kissed her slowly, first one part of her mouth, then another, before covering it completely with his own. Though passion beat strongly within him, aching to be free, this time he held it back and gave her all the love he felt instead. There was time enough for the other later. He had the rest of his life. Of their lives.

"Marry me, Liz." The words feathered softly against her mouth. "I need you. I need you to make me remember the sunshine."

"That sounds even better."

She let her jacket slip off her arms and she sank into the depths of the next kiss, a kiss that was far more urgent than its predecessor. The tree, she decided, had waited this long. It could wait a few hours longer.

In the background, coming from the CD player, someone was singing "Have Yourself a Merry Little Christmas."

Yes, Virginia, Liz thought, elated, just before all thoughts were wiped away, there *is* a Santa Claus. And he just made an early delivery.

* * * * *

COMING NEXT MONTH

#736 VIRGIN TERRITORY—Suzanne Carey
A Diamond Jubilee Book!
Reporter Crista O'Malley had planned to change her status as "the last virgin in Chicago." But columnist Phil Catterini was determined to protect her virtue—and his bachelorhood! Could the two go hand in hand...into virgin territory?

#737 INVITATION TO A WEDDING—Helen R. Myers
All-business Blair Lawrence was in a bind. Desperate for an escort to her brother's wedding, she invited the charming man who watered her company's plants...never expecting love to bloom.

#738 PROMISE OF MARRIAGE—Kristina Logan
After being struck by Cupid's arrow—literally—divorce attorney Barrett Fox fell hard for beautiful Kate Marlowe. But he was a true cynic.... Could she convince him of the power of love?

#739 THROUGH THICK AND THIN—Anne Peters
Store owner Daniel Morgan had always been in control—until spunky security guard Lisa Hanrahan sent him head over heels. Now he needs to convince Lisa to guard his heart—forever.

#740 CIMARRON GLORY—Pepper Adams
Book II of *Cimarron Stories*
Stubborn Glory Roberts had her heart set on lassoing the elusive Ross Forbes. But would the rugged rancher's past keep them apart?

#741 CONNAL—Diana Palmer
Long, Tall Texans
Diana Palmer's fortieth Silhouette story is a delightful comedy of errors that resulted from a forgotten night—and a forgotten marriage—as Long, Tall Texan Connal Tremayne and Pepi Mathews battle over their past...and their future.

AVAILABLE THIS MONTH

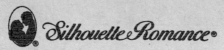

A duo by Laurie Paige

There's no place like home—and Laurie Paige's delightful duo captures the heartwarming feeling in two special stories set in Arizona ranchland. Share the poignant homecomings of two lovely heroines—half sisters Lainie and Tess—as they travel on the road to romance with their rugged, handsome heroes.

A SEASON FOR HOMECOMING—Lainie and Dev's story...available in June

HOME FIRES BURNING BRIGHT—Tess and Carson's story...available now

Come home to A SEASON FOR HOMECOMING (#727) and HOME FIRES BURNING BRIGHT (#733) . . . only from Silhouette Romance!

Diana Palmer's fortieth story for Silhouette . . . chosen as an Award of Excellence title!

CONNAL
Diana Palmer

Next month, Diana Palmer's bestselling LONG, TALL TEXANS series continues with CONNAL. The skies get cloudy on C. C. Tremayne's home on the range when Penelope Mathews decides to protect him—by marrying him!

One specially selected title receives the Award of Excellence every month. Look for CONNAL in August at your favorite retail outlet . . . only from Silhouette Romance.

CON-1

 *Diamond Jubilee Collection*

It's our 10th Anniversary...
and *you* get a present!

This collection of early Silhouette
Romances features novels written
by three of your favorite authors:

ANN MAJOR—*Wild Lady*
ANNETTE BROADRICK—*Circumstantial Evidence*
DIXIE BROWNING—*Island on the Hill*

* These Silhouette Romance titles were first published in the early 1980s
  and have not been available since!

* Beautiful Collector's Edition bound in antique green simulated leather to
  last a lifetime!

* Embossed in gold on the cover and spine!

✂ **PROOF OF PURCHASE**
